HURRICANE CANOE

AN ADIRONDACK WILDERNESS THRILLER

RICHARD M. BROCK

BOGIE ROAD PUBLISHING
DENVER

ℍB

BOGIE ROAD PUBLISHING
An independent publishing venture
www.richardmbrock.com
facebook.com/richardmbrockauthor

Published by Bogie Road Publishing, Ltd.
An imprint of Richard M. Brock
Denver, Colorado
Copyright © 2023 Richard M. Brock
All rights reserved.

Library of Congress Control Number: 2023907337

Names: Brock, Richard M., author
Title: Hurricane canoe : an adirondack wilderness thriller / Richard M. Brock.
Description: Denver : Bogie Road Publishing, 2023.
Identifiers: LCCN: 2023907337 (hardcover) | ISBN: 979-8-9878757-0-4 (hardcover) | ISBN: 979-8-9878757-1-1 (paperback) | ISBN: 979-8-9878757-2-8 (ebook)
Subjects: BISAC: FICTION / Thrillers / Suspense. FIC030000. : FICTION / Action & Adventure. FIC002000. : FICTION / Nature & the Environment. FIC077000.

Richard M. Brock's books may be purchased in bulk for promotional, educational, or business use. Please contact info@richardmbrock.com.

Cover design and photograph by Richard M. Brock
www.richardmbrock.com

ALSO BY RICHARD M. BROCK

Cross Dog Blues

Up a Tree

www.richardmbrock.com

To Pops

HURRICANE

CANOE

PROLOGUE | THE NEWS

ON A BRIGHT, late-summer afternoon in the Adirondack Mountains, at the far end of a secluded bay on Lake George, the television in the bar of the Sacrament Marina was tuned to the news, and no one was watching. Two men sat in one of the old wooden booths near the back of the room, hunched in animated conversation, and an old man lazily mopped the floor near a row of large open windows that looked out at the lake and the weathered wooden docks and the sun-splashed boats lined up in their slips. The boats rolled and clanged gently in the same pleasant breeze that drifted through the windows. The old man paused his mopping to smile.

With no one watching, the news anchor on the TV threw it to a rookie on a boardwalk somewhere on Long Island. The rookie propped himself theatrically against what looked to be little more than a breeze itself. A blue and gold New York State flag rolled flaccidly on a pole behind him.

"Thanks, Jan," the reporter shouted, grabbing his hat and mashing it against his head. *"After pummeling Bermuda, Hurricane Zebulon is lurking out there behind me right now, moving north. Most models have it staying out to sea and diminishing. But with the warmest waters on record in the Atlantic this summer, some say it could intensify one last time and even take a sharp turn northwest, running right over New York City."* Dramatic pause. *"And a secondary concern among some forecasters is a major system moving east over the Great Plains right now. If these storms were to collide, and if the hurricane behind me weakens just a little as it makes landfall, roughly equaling the power of the storm coming from the west, they could stop each other dead in their tracks. This would make for a prolonged period of exceptionally wet weather that could bring severe flooding to New York City and north—"*

The rookie continued his impassioned report on the small TV on the rough-hewn shelf in the corner of the Sacrament Marina, and his voice was carried away by the breeze, over the old man mopping, beyond the two men arguing in the booth, across the cool, dark waters of Lake George, and up into the dense and bewildering forest shrouding the slopes and peaks of the ageless Adirondack Mountains.

THE FIRST | STICKFISH

IT TAKES TIME, typically a long time, to acclimate to severe hardship. But the conscious realization of the depths of one's descent will often come in the blink of an eye. It came to Gilbert Willards at midnight of the thirteenth day, and when it did, the pain flashed from every wound on his body.

Thirteen days earlier, Gilbert stood on the dock of the Long Lake public boat launch with his belly pushed out in front of him. He was short, with receding hair matted forward and a bulky orange life preserver bunched over his short-sleeved plaid shirt. He stood with a hunched spine and his arms at his side because he didn't know what else to do with them. His chin jutted forward to match his belly and his meek smile was very kind and nervous from below icy blue eyes that flickered with an intensity unmatched by the rest of his being. Those eyes watched Trent Leno as Trent aggressively packed their gear into the canoe.

"That ought to hold 'er in there," Trent announced as he slapped the top of the last bag and stood up. He arched his back in a dramatic stretch that seemed more to show off his bulging pectoral muscles than to actually stretch anything. He paused there for a moment, preening like a Greek statue as he stared off at the mountainside. He wore a tight black t-shirt tucked into camouflage pants and sturdy hiking boots on his feet.

With a triumphant sigh, Trent turned back to Gilbert and slapped him on the back. "Gonna be a blast, eh Gilly?"

"Sure is," Gilbert agreed with a warm smile. But both he and Trent knew it was a lie, and that if either of them had a choice, this was the last place they would be.

Trent grinned and sprang nimbly into the canoe.

Then, with a great deal of effort and pacing along the dock, Gilbert managed to pour himself into the canoe, which shook and rolled and was only kept from tipping by Trent's sturdy hold on the dock's piling.

"*Phewww*," Trent joked from the back, clutching the dock as Gilbert lurched into place. "Like a *cat!*"

With shaking knees, Gilbert balanced himself on the narrow seat in the front of the canoe. It was his first time in a canoe like this, and only maybe his tenth time in a boat of any kind. He tried to see the bright side of the situation. But there wasn't one.

Gilbert chuckled nervously back to Trent and picked up the paddle.

As they glided toward the open waters of Long Lake, Gilbert could feel Trent's eyes on his back. When he looked back from time to time, Trent made the paddling look so easy, stabbing the dark wooden paddle into the water and tearing it backward over and over in a metronomic rhythm.

But Gilbert's paddle wobbled as he drew it back, or skimmed across the top of the water. With each stroke, the front of the canoe drifted toward whichever side Gilbert was paddling. Then Trent would shout "*Switch!*" and they would switch sides, and the canoe would swing back the other way as Trent's paddling overpowered Gilbert's. Like this, they zig-zagged past the homes and camps on the south end of Long Lake and were soon into the waters of the undeveloped northern portion of the lake.

Gilbert became more comfortable after the first hour, and by the end of the second hour, they had covered over six miles and were following a much straighter course.

About an hour later, as they drifted across the opening to a small cove on the forested, east shore, Trent hollered, "Let's drop a line, see if the fish are biting."

"Okay," Gilbert agreed.

Trent pulled the fishing poles from their resting spot on the side of the canoe, and his tackle box from under his backpack.

"You do much fishing, Gilbert?"

"A little, when I was a kid. Not really anymore."

"Well, no worries, my man. We're in the same boat. I'm about as bad a fisherman as exists. I think I get it from my grandfather. I don't think I ever saw that man land a fish, but he'd go out every weekend."

"Not about the fishing then?"

"Amen to that."

"My grandfather was a fisherman, too," Gilbert said. "Not, like, as a job. Just for fun. I only met him a couple of times—he lived in Montenegro—but they tell me that he'd go out just about every day. Mostly just to drink vodka and get away from my grandmother, they say."

"Ha! You said it." Trent chuckled and fed himself some line. "Speaking of, how do you think the sisters are doing?"

Gilbert paused and looked out at the lake. "Shopping in Manchester this time of year. They must be having fun."

"With their parents?" Trent said and raised his eyebrow.

Gilbert chuckled. "Their parents are all right."

"All right?" Trent spouted. "My goodness, Gilbert, they're not listening, you know. We're out here on this lake all by ourselves." He looked right at Gilbert as he said it. "I'm not wearing a *wire*, you know."

Gilbert grinned uncomfortably, eyeing Trent. "No, really," Gilbert said. "They've always been pretty good to me."

"Well, they would, wouldn't they," Trent agreed and looked off with a sigh. "That's just because you're married to Jeannie, and she's not crazy. They've been at my neck since the first date Liz and I went on." Trent grinned. "That family."

Gilbert smiled nervously and palmed his hair forward.

"Ah, who knows?" Trent said with a grunt as he fed some fishing line through the eye of a hook. "Maybe I'm just an asshole."

Gilbert chuckled. Despite his tension and nervousness about being in the canoe—and out there with Trent—the sun was warm on his back and the steady rocking of the canoe over the waves was relaxing.

"You're not jumping to refute that possibility, Gilbert," Trent said with a grin. "Is there something I should read into that?"

"No, no. I'm sorry. I wasn't trying to—"

Trent laughed in a jovial roar. "Relax, Gilly, I'm just busting your chops. Here." He handed Gilbert a fishing pole with a long purple rubber worm freshly skewered by a hook tied to the line. The worm had glitter of some sort mixed into the rubber and it flickered in the sunlight.

Gilbert took the fishing pole and held it out with the rubber worm just touching the water, waiting for Trent to bait his own line. Despite knowing generally how to cast and what to do, he waited for Trent to make the first move, as if to learn.

"You know, Gilbert, I didn't think in a million years you would agree to come out here."

Gilbert just smiled.

"I'm serious." Trent pulled his line taut to tighten the knot and bit off the remainder with his teeth before tossing the lure out into the lake. He closed up the tackle box and shook out his hands before snatching up his fishing pole and beginning a step-by-step demonstration for Gilbert. He showed Gilbert how to hold the line with his finger, release the reel, and cast the lure out into the lake at the edge of the weed line.

Gilbert watched, unoffended by the demonstration. His grandfather had taught him how to cast during one of Gilbert's visits to his small, stone home in the mountains of Montenegro when Gilbert was a kid, and he'd fished a few times since—but it had been a long time, and the gear was different, and he was happy to let Trent show him again. He practiced a few times, and Trent critiqued until Gilbert got the hang of it. Then Trent allowed himself to concentrate on his own line.

Trent cast his line out over and over, drawing it back in jerking motions offset by moments of stillness for the lure to slither enticingly down to the bottom. Gilbert studied Trent between his own casts and then tried to mimic what he saw.

Like this, they floated silently up the shore, a warm southern breeze nudging them north. At a grassy point, sometime later, Trent flicked his wrist and the purple worm danced through the air, landing with a plop right beside a downed tree reduced to just a trunk decaying in the lake. Immediately, as the worm landed, Trent focused intensely on the tip of the pole. He nudged the tip back and stared at it as if it were talking to him.

Then, in a flash, he jerked the pole backwards into the air, and the tip bent over in a deep arch. The reel whirled and whined, and the line danced about in the water as the fish took off with the lure. He let the fish run for a moment and then drew the pole back steadily, like an archer drawing his string, until his back was stretched as far as it would go and the tip of the pole was almost behind his head. Then suddenly, he dropped the tip in a flash, straight out in front of him, while at the same time, he reeled in the line for everything he was worth. When he had gathered all the slack out of the line, he began to draw the pole steadily back again. He did this over and over, and when the fish got in close to the canoe, it took off and ran again, and the reel whistled and spun as it surrendered line, before Trent pulled the pole steadily back again.

Gilbert gawked from the front and jumped in his seat from excitement when the fish burst out of the water like a missile and somersaulted at the end of the line, its tail flapping madly and the sunlight dancing off its wet flanks.

When Trent finally pulled the large bass into the canoe, he immediately jammed his thumb into its gaping mouth, yanked out the hook with his other hand, and hefted the fish above his head by the lower jaw, proclaiming, "DINNER!"

Gilbert had never seen anything like it in his life. "We're gonna eat that?" he asked.

"I told you I was bringing the food," Trent said. Then he picked a stringer out of his tackle box and opened one of the metal clasps and fed the wire through the mouth and out the gill of the fish, where he re-clasped it so the fish was tethered. He then hooked the end of the chain to the edge of the canoe and tossed the fish out into the water to swim alongside the craft.

"What is that for?" Gilbert asked.

"Keeps it alive until we cook it later."

"To make it fresh?"

"Yup."

Gilbert nodded and looked down at the fish, who swam along and seemed to at least be happy to be back in the water. *Relativity*, Gilbert thought and went back to fishing, his interest and excitement both spiked by the landing of the bass. He was almost having fun. He flicked his lure out into the waters and watched the line sit on the surface then finally relinquish, sinking below as it chased after the sparkly purple worm making its way down into the depths.

They sat silently for a long while, neither finding a need to talk. Trent seemed to be deep within his own thoughts as he continuously reeled in his line then cast it out again, over and over. The only sound was a slight breeze and a faint chatter of birds in the forest and the barely audible drone of a commercial jet passing over at thirty thousand feet. Gilbert breathed deeply and sighed.

The minutes drifted by in silence and Gilbert felt light, warmed by the sun in the crisp early autumn air.

But then he felt a soft nudge on his line while he was reeling in a cast. He froze mid-breath, pulling gently on the line until he felt another, stronger nudge. "I GOT ONE! I GOT ONE!" he screeched and yanked on the pole.

Trent was so startled by the sudden outburst that he jumped and nearly fell overboard. Gilbert pulled on the line and reeled as fast as he could, the reel whining as the line resisted. The canoe rocked and thrashed with the effort as Gilbert fought, and eventually the fish grew weak and the line slowly started coming in, and the reel whined less and pulled more. Gilbert reeled and reeled and tried to draw the pole back steadily and rhythmically like Trent had.

Beside him, Trent jumped forward on his knees and grabbed the net that was sitting in the middle of the canoe and thrust it aloft, ready to plunge it into the water and draw this beast from the darkness below. Gilbert focused straight out at the line and reeled.

Gilbert's arm grew tired, but he didn't stop reeling. And finally, a dark shape appeared from the blackness below and grew and grew. Gilbert nearly burst with excitement as he fought to draw it alongside the canoe.

Then he stopped reeling.

It was a long, thick, tangle of sticks and seaweed.

With the net stretched out over the side of the canoe, Trent tried for all he was worth to stifle his laughter as Gilbert stared in shock at the mass of twigs and lily pads floating to the surface along the side of the canoe. Trent had his head down, and his body was jerking with short grunts as he attempted to keep from laughing.

"It's not a fish," Gilbert stated as he stared down at the weeds.

"No," Trent let loose and burst out laughing. "It is *not* a fish."

Gilbert couldn't help but smile. "It put up a hell of a fight though," he said with a chuckle as he shifted his weight and combed his hair forward with the palm of his hand.

Trent slapped the side of the canoe and snorted with every other breath of laughter.

Gilbert chuckled.

"It happens to the best of us," Trent said, wiping his face.

They had a good giggle about the monster weed fish and talked about rock fish and stick fish, and soon, it was back to quiet and peace and sunshine—and whatever else was to come.

CHAPTER 2 | ROLL

SOMETIME LATER, AS they drifted along the eastern shore of a northern island, the canoe again erupted in excitement as Trent hooked another fish. A real fish. And this one put up a better fight even than the first, and Trent began to get very excited and shout things like "Whoa, Nelson!" and "It's a big one!" as he fought. When he drew the fish closer to the canoe, he took his hand off the pole to gesture madly to Gilbert as he yelled, "Grab the net! Grab the net! This is a big one."

Gilbert burst into motion and flailed his hands as his eyes darted desperately for the net. When Trent yelled for the net, Gilbert felt the same as he had back in gym class when he would be unlucky enough for the basketball to find him during the game and the more athletic kids would yell for him to pass it, right before it would be stolen away from him by the other team. He didn't like athletics. He couldn't stand the pressure. He was fine with pressure around a card table or a chess board, but not the pressure of sports, or any other display of physical aptitude.

But he tried to find the net.

Finally, Gilbert spotted it just as Trent pulled the fish alongside the canoe. It was huge. Gilbert grabbed the net, and in one motion, he lunged and thrust the net out into the water, just in time and right behind the enormous fish thrashing at the end of the line. He scooped, and the net encircled the fish, and as it did, Gilbert leaned over the edge of the canoe—too far. The canoe shifted, and the gunwale dropped below the surface of the water, and the whole vessel flipped over upside down, sending Gilbert and Trent splashing into the lake—where the fish remained—along with the net and all the other contents of the canoe.

Trent burst out of the water in immediate action. With his fishing pole still in hand, he grabbed a bag that was floating away and then a paddle. The fish had spit out the hook in the commotion and was gone into the depths of Long Lake. Trent spun his head to Gilbert. "Are you all right?" he yelled.

Gilbert flopped and thrashed and choked on the flying water as he panicked, holding onto his orange life-preserver for dear life. His eyes were as wide as saucers, staring at it all in unfocused shock.

"Come over to the canoe," Trent commanded with a steady voice as he swam toward Gilbert. "You can hang onto it."

Gilbert slowed his thrashing and composed himself as much as he could and had to remind himself that he knew how to swim—and that he had a life preserver on. Out of pure, panicked, seizure of muscles, he had gripped his fishing pole as he went overboard and he still held it with white knuckles. He doggie paddled toward the capsized craft bobbing in the water.

When Gilbert was halfway to the canoe, Trent reached him and helped him the rest of the way, speaking very calmly as he pulled him to the overturned canoe. When they reached the vessel, Gilbert latched on to the exposed hull and held himself as far out of the water as he could.

"Just hang on. I'll gather the gear," Trent instructed. He then swam off after one of the bags that floated away and the cooler that bobbed like an ice cube in the roiling water. The cooler had a latch on its cover and it was still secure, and the bag, all the bags, as well as the airtight tackle box, were floating nicely on top of the water.

Trent glided through the water like a frog, kicking his legs and pushing the cargo effortlessly in front of him, gathering the items either on or beside the canoe with each trip.

"Be thankful I had the foresight to put most of the gear in dry-bags," Trent said as he swam after a backpack. "Did you happen to have the same foresight?"

Frozen in terror and still clinging to the hull of the capsized canoe, Gilbert shook his head, his eyes wild.

"Didn't think so," Trent said and grabbed the bag he was after and started swimming back to the canoe. Along the way he hooked Gilbert's bag with his arm. "Not a big deal though," he assured Gilbert as he reached the canoe. "Most of the essentials should still be dry."

Then he moved Gilbert out of the way and lifted the edge of the canoe and rolled it back over, right-side-up. The canoe was still almost fully submerged.

Gilbert, regaining his senses, didn't understand what Trent was doing at first, especially as Trent started pushing and pulling the canoe back and forth like a mad-man, like he was furious at the canoe. Gilbert thought he'd lost his mind, but he also seemed to be doing it for a purpose, tipping the edge each time he pushed the canoe so the water sloshed out. And sure enough, in short order, he'd removed much of the water from the canoe and thrown the gear in. Then, with the now re-floated canoe, they began swimming the short distance to the small is-land in the middle of the lake. Trent kicked his feet smoothly and forcefully with one arm out in front, push-ing the canoe forward through the water while Gilbert held onto one of the tethered ropes and kicked his feet in a lurching, twitching motion along the side of the canoe, eye to eye with the first fish they caught, still on the stringer, who seemed to revel in the irony—but would still be dinner.

CHAPTER 3 | CAMP

Trent pulled the last bag out of the canoe and tossed it up with the others resting on the grassy shore. He opened the top of a large camping backpack and started pulling out dry-bags full of clothes and food and gear.

Gilbert sat shivering on the ground with a blanket around his shoulders and a dazed look in his eyes. Trent glanced over at Gilbert from the pile of soggy bags on the shore and then stopped what he was doing and stepped over and put his hands on his waist, sighing deeply. "Well, Gilbert, that fish sure fished us," he said after a moment, grinning. "Instead of coming into the boat, he dropped us in the water with him. Never seen anything like it." He looked down at Gilbert and chuckled, and Gilbert looked up at him and the slightest grin cracked his lips.

"Gilbert," Trent continued. "I think I just became the second worst fisherman in the world." He leaned down and slapped Gilbert on the back then sat down next to him and started untying his soaking wet boots. "I guess we'll be camping here then," he said as he assessed the situation. "On our own private island."

"I'm sorry," Gilbert said, looking around at the little island—not how he'd hoped this would go.

"Looks pretty damn good to me."

"And we still have the first fish that was tied to the canoe?"

"We still have the first fish. Yes, we do."

"The second one was a big one though, wasn't it?"

"Ha!" Trent shouted. "You got that one right, Gilbert. He was the mighty King Finnegan for sure."

*

TWENTY MINUTES LATER, once Trent finally wandered off to find firewood, Gilbert moved over to their gear and pulled up his sopping rucksack. With a glance back to make sure Trent hadn't reappeared, he opened the right-side pocket and reached inside.

Empty. It wasn't there.

His stomach lurched into his throat as he grabbed frantically at the other pockets. Maybe he'd accidentally put it in one of those. But he knew he hadn't. He knew exactly where it had been. Now it was not there. He spun and looked back the way Trent had gone.

But Trent was standing there, staring back at him from across the fire, an armload of sticks held in front of him. "Lose something?" he said with what could have been a hint of a smile.

Gilbert studied him—and couldn't tell. Had he taken it? Had it fallen out when the canoe tipped? Had Trent found it when he was gathering the bags in the water? Did he know?

"No," Gilbert answered, turning and closing the pockets and putting the bag back along the canoe.

Then suddenly, Trent was right behind him. Gilbert hadn't even heard him approach. "What the—?" Gilbert said, jumping, despite himself.

Trent grinned, seeming to enjoy the moment. But then he softened up and pointed at the bags and the bear canister, packed with their food. "We need to pack those under the canoe before bed," he said. "Just in case any critters take interest."

Gilbert exhaled and looked down at the bags. "Yeah, —yeah," he said and stood up, making way for Trent to grab the bear canister. "You think there are animals on this little island?"

*

FOUR HOURS LATER into the night, after dinner and after the gear was stowed under the canoe, Trent sang like a pirate as he danced around the fire with the one thing he left out of the bear canister: his bottle of rum. Gilbert watched.

"We will take our restitution from the gills of the King! Off with the head of the mighty King FINNEGAN!" Trent slurred. *"We will take our restitution from the gills of the King! Off with the head of the mighty King FINNEGAN!"* He pulled from the neck of the bottle of rum and wiped his mouth with the back of his forearm, and then continued around the fire.

Gilbert, now warm in dry clothes beside the roaring fire, watched Trent with a nervous smile.

"It's a wild world we live in, Gilbert," Trent said during a lull in his dancing, stopping to slug the rum and stare into the fire.

Gilbert nodded his agreement and sipped the rum in his tin cup, also looking down at the fire but watching Trent out of the corner of his eye. Was Trent getting his nerves up? Liquid courage? Or was he just getting drunk? Gilbert wore a set of white, long-john underwear and shirt provided by Trent from one of the water-sealed bags. He wore dry wool socks—also from Trent—and no shoes and had a blanket hung over his shoulders.

"A wild, wild world. Did you know that one-point-two-five million people die in car accidents every year?"

Gilbert palmed his hair forward and looked into the fire.

There was a long pause as they both stared at the fire.

"Do you really love Jeannie, Gilbert?" Trent said suddenly, turning to Gilbert, his eyes darkening.

"Of course," Gilbert said, surprised at the abrupt inquiry.

"Smart boy."

Gilbert didn't know what to make of it, and Trent stared him down for a long minute, Gilbert watching the fire, waiting for whatever might come.

Finally, Trent turned and spat. "But I call bull."

Gilbert's eyes narrowed.

"Way I see it, love is just a convenient lie."

"Love?" Gilbert said.

"Love," Trent said, as if the word itself were rotten.

Gilbert looked at the ground.

"And you love being *married* to her?"

"Yeah, of course," Gilbert said. "I know marriage isn't for everybody, but I like it. It suits me."

Trent raised an eyebrow and spit again.

"What's this about?" Gilbert said, sitting up and looking across at Trent.

"Just asking you how you like marriage, is all."

"Yeah?"

"Yeah," Trent said and kicked at a branch in the fire, sending sparks rising up into the cosmos.

Gilbert palmed his hair forward. "I do," he said, still eyeing Trent, but sitting back. "I don't really like people too much, you could say, and Jeannie and I have a nice little thing going, I guess, where we can just mostly keep to ourselves. So, it works."

"Keep to yourselves, huh?"

There was a long pause, and Gilbert nodded.

"Smart boy," Trent slurred again and drank from the rum.

Gilbert palmed his hair forward.

A moment of silence passed. Then, from across the fire, Trent looked directly at Gilbert. "I was thinking about marrying Liz," he said, his face smiling, but almost turning to a snarl at the same time.

Gilbert looked down at the ground and pulled his tin cup to his lips.

Trent eyed him for a long moment, then turned his glossy gaze up toward Santanoni Peak, black in the eastern sky. "Who knows," he said.

Gilbert sipped from his cup and held it at his lips, staring at a single rock in the fire ring.

Trent was drunk, and after a pause, he snarled and spat into the fire and spun around, laughing and screaming up into the sky. "*Off with the head of the mighty King Finnegan!*" he sang in a raspy shout at the stars as he danced around the fire. He laughed and slapped Gilbert on the back as he went by, continuing his display around the fire, drifting in and out of the first layers of darkness as he went around and around, dark, light, dark, light.

An hour later, Trent lay on the ground beside the fire, looking a little green as Gilbert got up and added some wood to the fire.

"How's the sleeping bag? Dried out yet?" Trent asked without looking at him, slurring his words.

Gilbert stepped over and felt the cold, wet bag hanging from a rope strung between two trees. He shrugged. "Yeah, sure."

CHAPTER 4 | MORNING

GILBERT LAY AWAKE and shivering in his damp sleeping bag, clutching his knife and waiting for the sun to climb over the Santanoni mountain range.

The sky was lightening with the coming dawn and he knew the sun had to appear very soon, bringing with it its warmth and wakefulness. But the massive Santanoni range delayed its appearance even as the rest of the sky brightened.

Gilbert glanced over at Trent, asleep in his sleeping bag across the fire ring, then stared again at the top of Santanoni Peak.

Finally, the first rays rolled over the mountain and within ten minutes the sun was shining warm upon Gilbert's face and his damp sleeping bag. The bag steamed as the sun baked its outer shell. Gilbert sat up and leaned his face toward the sun, closing his eyes and soaking up the rays.

After the chilly night, it felt amazing, recharging. Maybe everything would be okay.

Trent had slept the whole night and was snoring in his bag. A splattering of vomit in the grass by the fire seemed to suggest that the rum had not agreed with him.

After ten minutes of direct sunshine, Gilbert got out of his sleeping bag and rubbed his hands together and hopped to warm up, making his way to his clothes hanging by the smoldering fire ring to see if they had dried. They were damp but manageable and he quickly put them on and rubbed his hands together. The clothes, though chilly, were warmed by the morning sun and then by his skin. Eventually, they even began to fully dry and he loosened up and started to feel alive again.

While Trent snored, Gilbert broke up some of the wood they had gathered the night before. Warmth still rose from the gray bed of the fire. He used the end of a stick to stir down into the ash, finding some dimly glowing red coals below.

Gilbert exposed as many of the coals as he could, then grabbed a handful of the birch bark that was left over from when Trent had started the fire the night before. Gilbert had never started a campfire before, but he'd watched TV, and Trent said that the birch bark was just like paper. Gilbert put the bark directly onto the glowing coals and then piled very small twigs on top of it and started to blow gently, like he had seen Trent do the night before.

After only a few breaths the birch bark caught and was soon burning intensely and transferring its charge to the sticks on top of it. Gilbert placed some larger kindling onto the flaming sticks and then some small branches, and within a few minutes he had a roaring fire going. He squatted down beside it and held his palms out to the flame and felt okay at that moment.

"Agghhhhhhhh," Gilbert heard from behind him. When he turned, he saw Trent rolling over in his sleeping bag. Trent rubbed his face and groaned and looked altogether in pain from hangover. "What the fuck are we—?"

Gilbert stepped back to give Trent space.

"Oh, fucking shit," Trent groaned and rocked back and forth, but as he awakened and became aware of his surroundings, he suddenly snapped his head around to Gilbert, his eyes narrowing.

Gilbert just muttered, "Good morning," and stepped back to the other side of the fire ring, giving Trent time and space to wake up.

Trent didn't say anything, but eventually he unscrewed his eyes and blinked long and sleepily twice as his flickering gaze dropped to the fire.

Gilbert poked the fire with a stick.

"You got a fire going," Trent stated after a moment. He swung his legs around toward the fire, still in his sleeping bag. His eyes were red and squinting, his hair a mess.

Gilbert shrugged his shoulders.

"Well, I'll be," Trent said, cracking a smile and rubbing his swollen eyes. "How'd you sleep?"

"Great," Gilbert lied. "You?"

"The sleeping was great. It's the waking up that hurts."

Gilbert chuckled and watched Trent gather himself and wobble to his feet.

"Where's the water?" Trent asked as he swayed back and forth, and then found his canteen and took a long drink. When he had finished, he stepped up beside Gilbert and admired the fire. "Nicely done, Gilly."

"Thanks. The coals were still there though."

"All the same."

Gilbert nodded and they stood and watched the fire for a long moment.

"So," Trent said and slapped his hands together. "What say we catch the morning rise?"

"The what?"

"Do some fishing."

The smile disappeared from Gilbert's face.

"Gotta go land the mighty King Finnigan, Gilly. Remember? He's right out there."

Gilbert matted his hair forward with the palm of his hand and stared at the fire.

"And, besides, we've got to get back in the canoe at some point, Gilbert. We're on an island, and they're not sending a chopper to pick us up."

Gilbert looked at the canoe resting in the tall grass beside the water. He had been trying not to think about having to get back into it.

"Hey, it'll be fine, buddy," Trent assured him with a grin. "Now you know exactly what *not* to do in a canoe."

Gilbert chuckled feebly but felt like throwing up.

"Let's eat a little breakfast and pack up. Then we'll go find a nice quiet cove and cast a couple of lines to get you comfortable in the canoe again. How's that sound? And I promise I won't ask you to net any fish."

Gilbert smiled and stared at the fire. There wasn't much getting around having to get back into the canoe. About that, Trent was right. "Okay," Gilbert finally agreed, with no other choice.

Over the next hour, they puttered around and packed up their gear and loaded it into the canoe. Most of the gear was dry by the time they packed it. The only things they left out were the cooler and the mess kits, and with them, Gilbert cooked up some bacon and eggs over the fire as Trent packed the canoe, and they ate heartily.

After breakfast, they finagled Gilbert into the canoe, and Trent shoved them off and hopped into the back, and they were out on the water again.

CHAPTER 5 | FISHING

THE SPARKLING SUNSHINE danced off the first fluted ripples skittering across the lake under the calm breath of the new day as they paddled to a cove on the west side of the lake so they could stay in the sun. Despite the lingering queasiness in the pit of his stomach, Gilbert felt himself relax—except for the times when Trent thought it would be funny to rock the boat suddenly to see how Gilbert would react. Soon they had their fishing lines in the water and were silently waiting for a strike.

As the waters of Long Lake rolled under their canoe, the sun became warm and Gilbert slouched down into his seat. He might have fought it, but the sky was blue and inviting, and the trees and grasses were fragrant in the air, and the birds fluttered and fought overhead, dancing and stalking, eating the morning's mosquitoes and singing out into the forest. The land and the water drew stark contrasts to each other: one open and smooth, but liquid, susceptible to the rising wind; the other solid and immutable, but softened by vegetation. Dark blues against vibrant greens, yellows, and reds. He looked up, and the flawless sky held and anchored everything below it, its bright blue immensity seeming to offer comfort and protection—joy even.

Gilbert stared at the sky, and from the corner of his eye, he saw Trent follow his gaze and study the same blue emptiness and cotton puff clouds.

"Rough day one in the wild, huh?" Trent said.

Gilbert chuckled and combed his hair forward with the palm of his hand. "I thought it was fun."

"Ha," Trent grunted.

"I did."

"You know, Gilbert, for a professional poker player, you don't lie so well."

Gilbert shrugged and cast his lure out into the water. "It was all right."

"You're getting closer."

The lake was calm as they drifted in their canoe, casting and reeling, casting and reeling—and eventually, they reached the far northern tip of Long Lake, where a river fed into a bay.

"Want to go catch some Brookies upriver?"

Gilbert felt a cold shiver run down his spine, but he just shrugged. He didn't want to go anywhere but home. But he knew he couldn't. So he took a deep breath and nodded and tried to lean into the calming repetition of the paddling.

"Push right up the middle," Trent instructed. "Doesn't have much flow down here."

They were leaving the open waters of the lake and passing into the buzzing, beating, chattering soul of a desolate Adirondack wilderness, where a mysterious and deceptive forest cloaked jagged mountain peaks and sheer river gorges. Nothing west for miles. Nothing north for miles. Nothing east for many, many miles. From here, the only connection back to the outside world was the long, dark length of water flowing out behind their canoe, slithering into the northern reaches of Long Lake. *"Here be monsters!"* the old maps said over this blank spot in northern New York. This way you do not go. The sounds of frogs and birds and critters of all shapes and sizes filled in behind their vessel as the open emptiness of the lake drifted away, narrowing into that echoing cacophony of sound.

Like this, they paddled for a long time, up the splintering and narrowing flow until the river became little more than a creek.

CHAPTER 6 | LEAN-TO

GILBERT CAME OUT of a quiet half-reverie as they rounded a curve in the river creek and both saw a sturdy, brown structure a short distance up from the water's edge: a three-sided Adirondack lean-to. The old, moss-covered lean-to seemed to call out to weary travelers: "*Come, friends, and make use of my shelter and warmth and safety. Have a fire in my pit, friend. Cook those lovely fish you have there. Find calm anchorage in the lee of my beach and pull up your vessel. Stretch your legs, good friends of mine. Find refuge under my roof and lie upon my planked floor. Find comfort within my three walls, for who among us needs four?*"

"This is nice," Gilbert said as they ran the canoe up the beach. They didn't even discuss landing. It just seemed a natural place to stop.

"Damn right it is," Trent said, jumping from the canoe right down into the water.

Gilbert couldn't resist the charm of this safe harbor in the dark forest. The lean-to sat a few paces up from the water on a large piece of exposed earth and granite bedrock. Trees huddled around it like cold soldiers of some forgotten war, warming themselves around a fire on a late winter's battlefield. Brown painted logs stacked on the back and along the two sides of the structure held a shingled roof that started near the underbrush in the back and ran up to a peak and down to an awning about seven feet from the ground over the open front. The shelter was designed to be ever open, so the beauty could pass both ways.

Inside, past a well-constructed fire ring, Gilbert could see the floor was time worn, with rough-hewn lumber floorboards built up off the ground on thick logs. Each corner of the structure was set on a solid fieldstone to make it all level. On a shelf in the front left side of the lean-to was a fishing lure and some line and a black and white Mead composition journal in a plastic bag and some matches and fire-starter cubes. All along the walls were initials carved into the wood alongside nails and hooks for hanging shirts and jackets and pots and pans.

Gilbert gazed in wonder at the idyllic little lean-to with its bright green moss growing up the back side and its thick, heavy, timbered sturdiness, a dry and sheltered island in an otherwise imposing forest.

"I present, the Adirondack lean-to," Trent said, waving his hand as he set a load of gear down beside the shelter. "But for our swim yesterday, we would have stayed in one of these down on the shore of Long Lake last night."

"They have a lot of these?"

"They're all over the Adirondacks. For anyone."

"Who takes care of them?"

"A lot of them have people who adopt them and take care of them. They're all a little different. Some are big and well taken care of. Some are old and little. Some have lots of useful stuff on their shelves, and some are bare. This one seems to be somewhere in the middle. If you grab that journal right there," he nodded to the shelf in the lean-to, "it'll probably tell you who takes care of this one."

Gilbert stepped over to the shelf.

"Almost all of them have one of those journals for people to write a little something in," Trent said, tossing his sleeping bag into the shelter. "Lets you know if there's a bear or something like that that's been lurking around other campers here."

"Really?" Gilbert said and lifted the journal and thumbed its pages. There weren't many entries. Most were from groups of friends out camping, and a few hardy families. It was a spooky place, way out in the wilderness, and no one had been that far up in a week.

Gilbert flipped through and didn't see any mention of bears—until he found an entry from the winter before.

A group of guys had stayed there the previous winter and said they heard something that almost sounded like a cat but was probably a bear out early from hibernation. They thought maybe its den was close by and they'd disrupted its slumber. They said they first heard it on the hike in, as they approached the lean-to, then periodically throughout the night. They were doing a variation of the Northville-Placid trail through the old Gooley Club and the Chain-Of-Lakes, camping in the snowy forest and snowshoeing across the lakes up to the great Goodnow Flow, ice fishing as they were hungry, sleeping when they were tired, making use of the various lean-tos. They said the snow was deep and windblown across many of the lakes and the coyotes were active at night, howling into the cold.

They had been out for two weeks when they signed that log book, arriving at the lean-to after traversing the Santanoni range. They said they were going north, into the frozen emptiness of the High Peaks region. They had dropped their resupply in advance and picked it up as they crossed the highway west of Newcomb, along the wooded banks of the juvenescent Hudson River. From there, they had snowshoed up an unplowed dirt road and across Newcomb Lake by old Great Camp Santanoni and then up over the top of the Santanoni Ridge to avoid any late-winter icy crossings on the many creeks and swamps between Long Lake and the Santanoni Range. They hoped to emerge from the wilderness near Lake Placid in a week or so—or, they joked, never at all if they could find a cabin by a lake like Walden, with fish and deer and no humans.

Gilbert looked at the signatures and pictured the four men, out there in the middle of nowhere, bundled in winter gear, on snowshoes, sleeping in this old lean-to and joking with each other as they scrawled in this very logbook, doodling a view from inside: their fire pit dug deep into the snow under the awning; pillows of snow hanging on the evergreen trees; the bare hardwood trees just a screen without leaves; the colorful sky showing through the creeping branches even in the pencil sketch; the creek cutting through the snow drifts in a black line; the campers and the campfire rising out of the ice and snow as living lead shadings. Gilbert looked out and tried to picture it with snow, with all the beautiful green leaves vacant from the trees and the ground covered in a deep layer of white. It was hard to even imagine at that time of year.

"Have you ever been out here in the winter?" Gilbert asked Trent.

Trent was back down at the canoe, grabbing more gear. "Not here specifically. But every winter I come out camping in the Adirondacks at least a few times and usually stay in a lean-to like this.

"Ever been ice fishing?"

"Yeah."

"You like it?"

"It's fun if you have enough whiskey and reefer and thick enough boots," Trent said with a grin as he brought up the bear canister with their food and mess kit.

"I don't get it," Gilbert said, shaking his head.

"It's an acquired taste," Trent conceded, then nodded at the notebook. "When you're done with that, grab the fish, Gilly. We're eating like kings tonight."

Gilbert smiled and set the notebook down and stepped down to the canoe to get the fish. At the canoe, he stopped for a moment and looked out at the forest, letting his mind go, almost enjoying it. The forest was quiet and haunting, but in a comforting way, in a way that made Gilbert feel like a small animal on the big surface of the world, in the big reaches of the wilderness, helpless but harbored. No buzz of the TV. No cars or traffic. Just a forest and a river and four fat fish on a steel stringer— and another human. Gilbert allowed himself to smile as he reached down and picked up the fish, feeling like a mountain man. Jeannie would laugh if she could see him now.

He shook his head. What the hell was he doing out here?

"Haul 'em up, Gilbert," Trent hollered down with a smile. He had a fire started already, a small flame flirting with the dried grass, birch bark and twigs in a ball at the center of the fire pit. As the flame spread, Trent gently placed larger and larger twigs, sticks, and logs onto the fire until it roared from the fire pit. "We'll let that right side burn down and be cooking in no time," he said as he stood up.

Gilbert brought the fish up to the fire, and they cleaned them and cooked them and ate them. They ate, and in Trent's case drank, like kings that night, as Trent had promised. They ate till they were full—and then kept eating and then ate some more and some more. It was a feast to be remembered and by nine o'clock, they both lay comatose by the warm fire with bellies full of fish and snacks and cookies and rum.

When they couldn't stuff another bite, Trent stood up unsteadily and patted his belly. "If we're done," he said and belched, "I'll pack everything up." Then he slowly and methodically scratched himself all over for a full two minutes as only a grossly overfed human alpha can, yawning and burping and otherwise endeavoring to somehow digest all the food he'd just engorged.

"Are you really worried about bears?" Gilbert asked as he, slightly more quietly, stretched himself out so his stomach could occupy better space inside his frame.

Trent shook his head and yawned. "No. Not really. The fire should keep them away, and even if they come sniffing around, they'll only be interested in the food, and that'll be in the bear canister."

That didn't make Gilbert feel a lot better, but he got up and helped Trent gather everything down to the canoe.

They packed the food back into the bear canister, and put it, along with their packs and all the rest of their stuff, under the overturned canoe on the little beach, safely away from where they were sleeping—they hoped.

"You think that will help?" Gilbert said as they

walked back up to the fire, his anxiety starting to grow as it got dark and they got ready for bed—and with the mention of bears.

Trent smiled drunkenly over at Gilbert, seeming to enjoy his nervousness. "We don't have to worry about bears, Gilly."

Gilbert nodded and palmed his hair forward, looking into the fire.

CHAPTER 7 | THE RISE

GILBERT WOKE WITH a start. His mind didn't immediately register where he was. An instant frantic confusion spiked his adrenaline, and he wrenched his arms loose of his sleeping bag, not knowing why he was confined. He was clutching his knife still, and all he could see were wood timbers, and all he could hear was a voracious roar that sounded like a jet engine. He jerked his legs and tried to free himself as the sound devoured his thoughts, making his head swirl. It took him a full ten seconds to finally come to and understand that he was in the woods in a lean-to, camping—with Trent.

He shook his head loose and looked over at Trent who had woken up with Gilbert's thrashing. He finally realized what the all-encompassing roar was.

Rain.

He'd heard the rain start up in the night. At the time, it was a calming patter landing on the roof that seemed harmless in and of itself, though its sound eventually defeated his attempt at wakefulness, lulling him into a deep and fitful slumber. Until now.

Gilbert took a few deep breaths to calm his beating heart and looked out the front of the lean-to, barely able to see anything through the sheet of water rushing off the roof. At first, he thought something was in his eyes, blurring his sight. The sheet was silver with a murky brown streak behind it that seemed to be moving very fast. As his eyes focused, he realized what the brown streak was: the river, the measly, creekish river, now risen up to the fire pit, racing by at the speed of a train.

"What the hell is that?" Trent asked and rubbed the sleep and hangover out of his own bloodshot eyes.

Gilbert just stared wide-eyed out the front of the lean-to.

"Is that the creek?" Trent asked in disbelief, popping up.

The wall of water coming off the roof made it impossible to get a clear view.

They both squinted as a blob of green moved down the middle of the brown rush outside, pausing twice and swinging around in a fluid dance beyond the curtain of rain. As Trent moved closer to the front of the lean-to, Gilbert saw through a momentary split in the curtain that the blob was a large tree being swept away by an ungodly torrent.

"That's a tree!" Gilbert yelped, fear washing away the last of the cobwebs in his head, bringing him to attention.

"The canoe!" Trent screamed. "What time is it?"

Gilbert sat wide-eyed. "Seven," he guessed.

"AM?" Trent said, frantically.

Gilbert just looked at him and then out at the water.

The canoe was gone, as was everything else.

"The rain wasn't supposed to get here till the afternoon," Trent said, his hands squeezing his head, staring at the water. "This is— Fuck."

"What—?" Gilbert muttered, staring out at the water, his eyes wide in disbelief. "What does this mean?"

Trent just shook his head absently and Gilbert looked down at his sleeping bag. All Gilbert had was his knife and what he was wearing to sleep in in his sleeping bag: sweatpants and a t-shirt. Luckily, he had kept his boots inside the lean-to when he went to bed the night before. But everything else was in his pack under the canoe, to keep it *safe*.

And indeed, the bears had not attacked them in the night.

"Was your pack under the canoe, too?" Gilbert asked over to Trent, though he knew the answer.

Trent just looked out at the water and scratched his head in frustration.

Gilbert shivered. This was bad news. And when he looked at Trent's corner of the lean-to, there was nothing, not even his boots. Gilbert scoured the four corners of the lean-to, and there were no boots. There was nothing.

"Were your boots out by the fire?" Gilbert asked, remembering Trent placing them by the fire the night before—to dry. It was after their feast and after they'd stowed the rest of their stuff. He was stumbling from rum by then, and Gilbert had watched from his sleeping bag and worried he would fall in the fire. His pants were already hanging by the fire from a stick set in the ground by that point. He had been in his boxers and undershirt, singing again, and that's how he'd gone to bed—or passed out. Now Gilbert looked over at him in the lean-to and saw he was obviously fighting the fog of a killer hangover as he stared out in shock at the raging mass of water running over the ground half-way through the fire pit.

There were no boots by the fire, no pants, and only half the fire pit itself remained, from what Gilbert could see.

"Maybe some of it washed up downriver," Gilbert said.

Trent didn't say anything.

"We can check."

The creek was three times wider than it was the night before, and it was angry. The dark brown water shifted and jumped and smashed into anything unfortu-nate enough to find itself in the path of the flood. A tree fought against the onslaught, remaining mostly vertical for a while, but slowly losing degrees to the horizon as it bounced back and forth, splitting the surface like a giant prow, being undermined every second, destined to be taken by the flood, a life well-lived.

Gilbert pulled himself out of his sleeping bag and the drop in temperature from the day before was immediately evident. He stepped on tippy toes to the edge of the lean-to floor, which was set back from the front eve by three or four feet. He stepped up to the edge, wiping the sleep out of his eyes, hoping to see the bags or the canoe hung up on a bush or tree. But all he saw was water running down, down, down, nothing in the world that could stop it.

"I don't see anything."

Trent just stared out the front of the lean-to.

CHAPTER 8 | FAMILY

IT WAS A little less than a year earlier that Liz first brought Trent around.

Gilbert and Jeannie were at Liz and Jeannie's parents' house in Glens Falls. It was an upstate autumn night in the finest form. The leaves had turned a few weeks before and now they littered the street, only the strongest remaining on the trees. It was football Sunday, and the Bennett family was watching the Bills.

"Fucking refs," Bob Bennett scoffed at the TV, shaking his head and looking over at Gilbert.

"Bob!" Joan Bennett scolded from the hallway.

Gilbert just shrugged his shoulders, turning up his hands.

"Joan!" Bob yelled out to his wife. "Grab Gilbert a beer." He nodded to Gilbert.

"Don't listen to him, Mom," Jeannie called out to her mother. "I'll grab him one in a minute."

"I don't need anything— from either of—" Gilbert said down to the carpet, trailing off.

They all heard the front door open and then slam closed.

"Don't slam the goddamn door!" Bob hollered without looking.

"Sorry, sir," came a voice they had never heard.

They all stopped and looked over as Liz walked in with a guy they'd never seen.

"Don't be a jerk, Dad," Liz said with a smile.

Bob Bennett craned around in his chair to see the newcomer.

"Everybody, this is Trent," Liz said, presenting him.

"He's a Bills fan at least," Bob said without smiling, seeing the Bills shirt Trent wore for the occasion.

"Goodness, Bob," Joan said from the entryway, moving over to Trent with her arms out.

"I'm just kidding," Bob said with a half-smile and stood up. "Pleased to meet you," he said and shook Trent's hand after Joan had given Trent a hug.

Gilbert and Jeannie stood. Gilbert shook Trent's hand and mumbled a hello, never looking up from the floor. Gilbert didn't like meeting new people. He had enough anxiety being around people he wanted to be around, people he'd known for years. New people were just too much most of the time.

"Well, not off to a good start, but we'll see," Bob said, waving a dismissive hand at the TV and sitting back down.

"Yeah, we were listening in the car on the way over," Trent said with a charming smile.

"Liz let you listen to football on the radio?" Bob said, leaning back in his recliner so he could bug his eyes up at Liz.

"Oh, shut up, Dad," Liz said, pushing him down in his chair from behind.

"I'm just saying," Bob said, chuckling and holding up his hands in surrender.

"I know you're just saying. Why don't you just *not* say—anything, for like two hours?"

"Okay, okay. Just glad my little Lizzie is so interested in football now."

"Shut up."

He just grinned, getting a kick out of her reddening cheeks.

"I know enough about football to know it's just a stupid game that grown men shouldn't care so much about," she said, then turned to Trent. "Sorry."

Trent just smiled. "Can't argue with that," he said.

"Oh, well," Bob said as if profoundly surprised, looking over at Trent. "You've already learned that then, huh?"

"What's that?"

"Can't argue with Lizzie."

"No, no," Trent said with another grin, directed at Liz, who visibly melted when she looked at him. "I wasn't saying that."

"Oh, you will be," Bob said.

"Jesus, Dad," Jeannie jumped in. Then she turned to Trent. "He's a little starved for attention, as you can see."

Trent just grinned and Bob held up his hands in surrender.

"What do you want to drink, hon?" Joan asked as she walked out into the kitchen.

"Anything," Trent said.

"Wine spritzer, then," she called back as she disappeared.

Trent just looked after her, confused, and Liz rolled her eyes.

"You guys are a riot," Liz said, unamused.

"So, what do you do then, Trent?" Bob asked.

Gilbert sat back into the corner of the couch and watched without appearing to watch, seeming to just look down at the floor. He was a poker player. A professional one. His job was to read faces. And there was something there in Trent's reaction to that question that made Gilbert pause.

CHAPTER 9 | MARINA

IT WAS MAY, about nine months after they first met Trent watching the Bills game. Gilbert stood in front of an old boat storage building at the back of the Sacrament Marina on Lake George. It had the smell of a marina: damp wood and fish mixed with gasoline vapors and a dusty dry rot. All of it came together to make Gilbert think of snakes. He was at the back of the marina. In front of him stood a giant steel building with three levels of dry boat storage. Fork lifts and tractors dotted the paths and roads between the parked boats and gas tanks and narrow, weedy canals at the back of the property. At first, he thought he'd taken a wrong turn. It was an odd place for a poker game. But then again, it was quiet and private, and that's what these guys were usually paying for.

He looked around, momentarily chilled. A marina can be a spooky place at night. These back sections can even be a little spooky during the day. As he moved down the tin-sided boat barn, he saw a large man, a bouncer, outside a metal door at the end. He had an earpiece. This was Gilbert's door.

"Donzi," Gilbert said to the bouncer, the password he'd been given by Jeff, his agent, so to speak. Jeff helped Gilbert find poker games, and Gilbert gave him a cut if a place worked out. He was usually good about getting Gilbert into games with harmless rich guys who just wanted a night out at the card table and were happy to lose more often than they won.

Tonight would be different.

The goon opened the door without a word and Gilbert stepped into a steel room with a door at the end. *The decompression chamber*, he thought. Every poker room had something of the sort, a walk you had to do before you entered the room with the game. Whether a restaurant kitchen, hotel suite, or casino floor, Gilbert considered it his changing station, his phone booth. He'd better get his head right in the time it took him to walk through that decompression room, however long it was and whether he was going in to play or coming out after having won or lost. He'd better get himself together in that time. Leave anything else at the door. There was no other way to play poker, in his opinion.

He knocked on the inner steel door there at the marina, and it was opened by another goon. He knew something was wrong when he saw this guy. He was huge and thick and wearing a half-unbuttoned flannel shirt over stained Carhartt dungarees. His massive hairy chest and growing belly stuck out in front of him and he chewed on a giant cigar in the side of his mouth. He was clean shaven and tan, with black hair pushed back absently. His smile was infectious, and deadly. This was Jimmy Dove. Gilbert knew Jimmy Dove all too well and had long been aware that Jimmy Dove ran poker games in the area. But Gilbert had always avoided those games—and as much of Jimmy Dove as he could—at all costs. It was a lot safer taking the equivalent of pocket change from businessmen in amusement games in Saratoga Springs than it was to sit around a table with a bunch of hardened mobsters. Jimmy Dove was a mobster—an upstate mobster, but a mobster all the same. His games were interesting, Gilbert had always heard, and could be profitable. But he was a mobster. Dangerous, any way you slice it.

What the hell had Jeff gotten him into?

"This is our pro!" Jimmy Dove said, grabbing Gilbert around the shoulders and turning him to the guys milling around the table. Half of them were straight out of central casting: fine suits and cuff links and perfectly imperfect pocket-squares with gray pompadour haircuts and big meaty faces that looked like they'd taken more than enough blows to warrant the mean countenance those blows created.

Gilbert glanced up and nodded. It was the best he could do. The other half of the people were some of their local counterparts like Jimmy Dove. These guys were gangsters all the same—they just didn't always look like it.

They took care of that particular far-gone satellite of crookery up in the Adirondack Mountains. Rural pots need skimming, too. Boonies or not. Plenty of raw fish flooded those little vacation towns in the summer, and someone had to be there to sop up the gravy. Apart from them, there were a couple of other guys Gilbert couldn't really pin at first inspection, but who looked like regular guys, probably local businessmen or hangers on, dancing with the Devil's tentacles up their skirts.

Shit, he thought. He needed a win tonight. The mortgage was due. But this was not the table at which to win. Not big. And he couldn't just leave. Not with these guys. These guys were true sharks of the rock. You make no sudden movements in their presence. If you're going one way and they don't kill you, keep going that way. So, he sat down.

He'd been at more than a few tables where he'd decided before he started playing that he had to lose, or at least not win big. It came with the territory for a professional poker player. Online poker and casino tournaments can be nice, but you have to have some cash games to pay the bills. And cash games that have a winning margin the poker player can live on can be hard to find, especially early in his career, before he has a network.

Gilbert knew it would be that kind of night. He hadn't had one of these in a long time. He'd gotten smarter since those early days trying to find decent games. Mobsters, by their nature, don't like to lose money.

Instead of winner take all, they prefer win *or* take all. They almost look at it like you're stealing from them if you win. Especially if it's a game of poker and you beat them on a tough hand and they look bad in front of their mobster friends. Then you might get a knock on your door the next day. Or maybe you won't. But, just like poker, you have to play the range: what might happen, what they could be playing. Then, is it worth whatever you have to throw in the pot? His and Jeannie's safety was not worth betting against the hope that one of these guys didn't take losing personally. It was percentages, and playing in mob games wasn't sustainable. Eventually even the low odds would come through. So, Gilbert stayed away from any game that even sniffed of illegality or criminal organizers or players. Hard to find, he'd often joked with Jeannie: a poker table in America without a bunch of crooks of one form or another around it. But it was a rule he was careful about. And yet, tonight he would sit at a table of hardened mobsters.

Before the game started, Gilbert drifted over to the seemingly makeshift bar of this boatshed barroom at the back of the Sacrament Marina, decorated with ropes and tackle from the docks. There was a television on a roughhewn wooden shelf in the corner, and it was tuned to the news. Below it, a man half sat on a stool, leaning against the bar, looking out at the room. Gilbert sat down next to him.

"Chuck," he said and nodded.

"How do'n, Gilbert?" Chuck said. Chuck was a do-all for Jimmy Dove and the northern Bogacci family, as far as Gilbert could tell, but Gilbert liked him all the same. He was quiet and unassuming, about forty-five or fifty, with intense, almost yellow eyes contrasted against light brown skin and short little dreadlocks over a heavy face, scarred from fights that Gilbert for some reason got the impression Chuck probably won but probably didn't even truly want to be a part of. He seemed very quiet, almost caring, but tough as nails. Gilbert found him fascinating, despite who he worked for. There were stories about how he'd learned directly from the fighting monks of Tibet when he was in his twenties. He drove for Jimmy Dove sometimes, and carried things that needed carrying, and knocked in teeth when they needed knocking, apparently, among other things.

"I can't complain," Gilbert said to Chuck, leaning against the bar.

"Thought you didn't do these games."

"I don't," Gilbert said, palming his hair forward.

As Gilbert already knew, Chuck wasn't big on small talk—and *was* big on discretion—so he didn't ask more but just nodded his head at Gilbert and looked around the room.

"Finally finished *Moby Dick*," Chuck said after a moment.

"No shit," Gilbert said, turning to him and grinning. "Weren't you reading that the last time I saw you—like, months ago?"

"That thing is long," Chuck said, chuckling. "Detailed. And makes you sleepy. It's hard to read it for long before you fall asleep. Soporific that is. But so good. So much information about whaling. What a crazy thing."

"Soporific?" Gilbert said, looking over as the door opened again and a new player stepped in.

"Makes you sleepy," Chuck said, wrinkling his forehead.

Gilbert grinned.

"What are you reading right now?" Chuck asked.

Gilbert never wanted to admit it, but he found it fascinating to talk literature with a guy like Chuck. It seemed so out of character. He almost looked homeless, if Gilbert was being honest, but he loved poetry and Dostoyevsky and Jack Kerouac. He said he read *On the Road* when he was a freshman in high school in the Bronx, and the next day, he tried to hitchhike to California but only made it to Jersey City.

Gilbert got to know Chuck through no choice of his own.

That first day at the Saratoga horse track started out looking like it might be one of those lucky days. Two of Gilbert's long shots had come in during the early races and he had a horse running in the day's top stake that was going off at ten-to-one. Gilbert had a good feeling—and a good tip—that it could win.

The horse won, and Gilbert thought it was his lucky day. He even called Jeannie and told her to put on her dress because he was taking her to dinner at the Adirondack Brewery, if she wanted to meet him there after her shift.

He was on the phone with her when he heard behind him, "Got some luck there, huh?"

He turned and met Jimmy Dove for the first time.

Jimmy Dove smiled his meaty smile. "I got me some folks with a farm down here by Saratoga Lake and they told me their horse was supposed to win," he said, scratching his sturdy belly and looking out at the track. He wore jeans and a long-sleeved Carhartt Henley t-shirt. In mob circles, Jimmy Dove ate at the far end of the table, but that didn't matter much to the general public in Jimmy's territory. A bat swung by a pawn hurts the same as one swung by a king. And Jimmy Dove was plenty mobster enough to warrant a broad berth.

"How'd you come to have that kind of money on that horse?" Jimmy asked directly, looking down at Gilbert's wager tickets.

Gilbert subconsciously pulled the tickets closer to himself and looked up at Jimmy Dove.

"Hel-*lo*?" Jimmy Dove said when Gilbert didn't answer right away.

"I just got lucky."

Jimmy Dove grinned at Gilbert. "I don't think you did."

"I—" Gilbert stammered and looked down at the floor.

"I'm not going to bother you," Jimmy Dove said with a smile. "I just want to know who your guy is."

"I— I don't have a guy," Gilbert lied.

Jimmy Dove's smiled stayed, but his whole face grew cold. "No, of course you don't," he said. "You just got lucky." And with that, he turned and waved to his entourage, which included Chuck, whom Gilbert had yet to meet, and they all walked away.

Gilbert watched them go, and even though he didn't know exactly who Jimmy Dove was just yet, his senses told him clearly who Jimmy *was* without his having to know. The way the seven other guys with him obeyed his command, and the way he looked over their heads, and over the heads of everyone there, made it clear this guy was accustomed to a certain level of acquiescence.

Knowing that, Gilbert had enough sense to know that their conversation had ended far too quickly for that to be the end of it. When he saw Chuck peel off from the group and make his way back, Gilbert honestly thought he might be in for some kind of beating. He thought about running, and looked around. But who was he kidding? At the time, he only knew Chuck as a nameless, rough-looking, middle-aged, black dude coming at him from the oddest mixed-gang of obvious hoodlums Gilbert could ever imagine. Chuck wasn't particularly tall, and was thick-faced and solid, but he still had that lightness of movement that immediately told Gilbert that fleeing was futile.

Gilbert braced, but, instead of a beating, when Chuck reached Gilbert, he just stuck out his hand for a handshake in a way that Gilbert would come to know as distinctly Chuck: humble and friendly, but stern and unwavering.

"My name is Chuck," Chuck said. "And that is Jimmy." He nodded toward the group of guys with Jimmy Dove at the center, laughing and waving his hands.

"Uh— Gilbert," Gilbert said and shook his hand.

"Jimmy says to meet him here tomorrow before the races," Chuck said. "And bring one of those lucky picks."

"I—" Gilbert started, but he didn't know what to say, so he just looked at Chuck and Chuck just nodded and walked away.

That was how Gilbert came to handicap horse races for the mob.

CHAPTER 10 | PONIES

CHUCK BECAME GILBERT'S mob handler, so to speak. He met Chuck once or twice a week for the rest of the season to give him horse racing picks. Gilbert knew some guys through World of Warcraft who worked in a few of the stables down at the track in Saratoga, and they always gave him good picks. He made a little money off of it, but it was more of a hobby or side project for him before he met Jimmy Dove and Chuck.

After closing day at the track that year, Jimmy—through Chuck—started asking Gilbert to come to his poker games. In the months from mid-September to mid-July, he didn't see any of those guys, but all through that winter, Chuck texted him about joining one of Jimmy's poker games. That first year, Gilbert just came up with excuses why he couldn't, but the next summer, one time when he was meeting with Chuck for the picks, he just came out and told Chuck that he didn't want to play in the poker games and why.

Chuck understood. Gilbert knew he would. He'd gotten to know Chuck well enough to feel comfortable telling him why he didn't want to play. And as expected, Chuck just let it go, and Gilbert never heard anything more about those poker games. He knew Jimmy wanted him there. People like Jimmy always want a professional at their games. It puts the game into the next level. Gilbert never asked, but he imagined that Chuck was the reason he didn't hear any more about it.

Chuck appeared to be one of the goons, at first inspection, like he was low on the totem pole, but as Gilbert observed Chuck around the other guys when he would sometimes run into the whole gang at the track, Chuck was always quietly on the outside of the group, and the other men showed him a level of respect in just how they moved around him and how they glanced at him for silent approval of something they said or did. It was hard to pin down, but there was a deference there that seemed above his ostensive rank.

Either way, Jimmy Dove never talked to Gilbert about poker again—until he walked into that boat warehouse at the Sacrament Marina, that night.

"I think Jimmy asked a favor of your buddy Jeff," Chuck said in a quiet voice to Gilbert as they sat at the bar, awaiting the poker game. "Don't blame Jeff. He didn't have a choice."

"Man," Gilbert said. "Why did he want me here so bad?"

"It's not about *so bad*," Chuck said. "It's just that he wanted you here. Little or a lot, Jimmy usually gets what he wants." Gilbert's face must have been hanging, because Chuck brightened up and patted him on the shoulder. "Don't stress it, Gilbert," he said. "It should be just this once. He just wants to impress his bosses with a big tournament-winning pro."

"His *bosses*?" Gilbert yelped.

"You know what?" Chuck said, grinning. "Let's forget about it. It's nothing. Just play the game, huh? Have fun."

"Yeah, fun," Gilbert said, palming his hair forward.

"I know what you're going to have to do," Chuck said, dropping his voice. "You've told me about games like these. But I couldn't do anything this time, so just look at it as the cost of doing business." He looked Gilbert right in the eyes. "And it's not every day you get to sit down with guys like these."

Gilbert nodded. "Who *are* guys like these?"

"Don't worry about it," Chuck said again, and grinned.

Gilbert sighed and looked around the room. The song *Summer Wind* by Frank Sinatra played in the background, and Chuck—much like most of the guys there—settled into a muted sway, drifting on his bar stool like the sailboats bobbing in their slips outside, rolling in the evening's remnants of the day's almost-summer wind behind the Sacrament Marina.

Gilbert tried to not think about who Jimmy's bosses might be, but ten minutes later, as they sat down and were introduced, the brooding old man sitting across from Gilbert was introduced as Salvatore. They didn't have to use his last name. Gilbert knew exactly who he was: Salvo Bogacci. *What the hell is Salvo Bogacci doing up here?* Gilbert thought. *Vacation?* And for some reason it was odd to think of the head of the Bogacci Family on vacation.

Gilbert won that night. Not much, and none of the big hands, but just enough, he hoped, to make himself unremarkable, forgettable. That pro that sat at their game once. What was his name? That's what he hoped.

As a whole, the evening was as unremarkable as can be expected while sitting around a table of hardened killers. But then, late in the night, Jimmy Dove turned from the table, throwing down his two cards to fold the hand. "Somebody call Trent and tell him to pick up some meats on the way," he said to one of his gofers. "I'm fuck-ing hungry."

Gilbert raised his eyes from the poker table and looked over at Jimmy Dove and the guy across the room he was talking to.

"What kind of meats?" the guy asked.

"Just fucking meats. I'm hungry."

The bouncer grumbled and turned to call, still looking plenty uncertain about what kind of meats he was supposed to ask for. If Gilbert hadn't been otherwise occupied by the comment itself, he might have wondered about the meats as well. It *was* rather vague. Cold cuts? Ribeye?

But Gilbert never learned the answer. He was gone before the meats, whatever they were, and whoever was bringing them, arrived.

CHAPTER 11 | OUT

"WE COULD CHECK downstream," Gilbert suggested, back in the lean-to. "Maybe some of the gear got hung up on something, or washed up onto dry land.

Trent sat in the same spot, expressionless, looking out at the water. But eventually, he nodded, and they got ready and set out into the rain. Trent was barefoot, in just boxers and a t-shirt. Gilbert had boots and sweatpants and a t-shirt. The rain was cold and harsh, dropping down from the sky with a ferocious disregard for anything below it.

They walked the bank of the river, hoping something had snagged on the quickly eroding banks.

They looked until what they estimated was noon and returned to the lean-to soaked, having found nothing.

"I wish this had happened after breakfast," Trent complained. Everything he had, apart from his t-shirt and boxers, had been washed away. "What I wouldn't do for some bacon and eggs right now."

Gilbert watched Trent and his mind raced. Both of their cell phones had been packed away in their gear. Not that they would help out here anyway. The closest cell coverage was somewhere around Saranac Lake, many miles to the north, or along Interstate 87, far to the east. "Is this like something like, like—survival?"

Trent thought for a moment and chuckled. "Nah, Gilly," he assured. "Just gonna be a long walk. We'll hike back. It won't be quick and it won't be easy, especially not in this rain, but up the river a bit we'll run into the North-ville-Placid Trail that goes back along the shore of the lake to the road. Maybe we'll even get lucky and the canoe will have made it to the lake and come ashore on the trail side."

Gilbert palmed his hair forward. "Fuck."

They decided to pack their sleeping bags into their stuff-sacks to keep them as dry as possible. They thought about using them over their shoulders like shawls, but de-cided that they could handle the rain for now, and the benefit of having a dry sleeping bag to warm up in if they got cold on the way out was worth the added chill right then as they started their hike.

It was not a cheery farewell as they left the lean-to. Somewhere down the rushing brown mass of water was all of their gear. Their food would now feed the fish they'd tried to catch and make into food the night before. And if they didn't get moving through this long hike out to safety, they might turn into a million tiny bites of fish food themselves.

They hiked up the river's edge, swampy and trail-less. The wind whipped through the forest and the rain poured down, and beside them, the creek-turned-torrent raged through its ever-widening course. The travel was slow and grueling.

They sank in up to their ankles in the saturated ground surrounding the swamp, which rose as if the earth might be swallowed up whole by the waters. They pulled themselves through sections by the branches of trees growing above the widening muck. They hopped along rocks any time they could find them. And they rested only when one of them was injured in any way: from a stick cutting Trent's bare foot or from Gilbert's slipping down a bank into a rock half-buried in the mud. At those times they rested only as long as it took to recover. They were both driven by the warmth and shelter of Trent's truck, waiting for them at the end of this grueling trek.

It took three hours of bushwhacking for them to cover the first couple of miles up to the Northville-Placid trail. They reached it in the late afternoon, and it was like heaven, wide and well-maintained, a common thru-hike that got plenty of use.

They caught their breath as they came out into the opening of the trail, their optimism growing with the clear path forward. They didn't lag at the junction, trying to cover as much ground in daylight so the final miles at night would be easier.

After a few minutes, Gilbert looked over at Trent

limping in his bare feet. "Why don't you take the boots for a bit?" Gilbert said. "They're probably small for you, but they might help. And the trail looks pretty well-packed so I don't mind going barefoot for a while. Give your feet a break."

Trent was obviously surprised. "That's a hell of a nice thing to offer," he said, looking over at Gilbert. "But I couldn't do that."

"No, no, really, I insist. Give your feet a break." He squatted down and began untying his shoes.

Trent furrowed his eyebrows and watched Gilbert untying the shoes. Gilbert pulled the boots off and held them up to Trent with a confederating nod. Trent took the boots and looked at them and then looked at Gilbert. The gift of a pair of boots from one person to another becomes an enormous gesture when the two persons find themselves stranded deep in the forest with only one pair of boots.

On the trail, he and Trent moved much faster and the rain even seemed like much less of a bother. For the first hour, everything proceeded well and their situation began to look up. They even tried to jog a bit—a very little bit.

But their spirits dropped when they heard Pine Brook long before they could see it. At a distance, it sounded only like a dull roar. But as they approached, the roar became a jet-engine and engulfed all other sounds.

The log bridge that was supposed to cross the

brook was long gone. Only its posts remained. The brook, which was normally about six to eight feet wide, was running over its banks in a twenty-foot swath. To attempt a crossing would be stepping into a blender.

They stared at the flow silently, though not even the loudest shout could have been heard over the rush of water anyway. Trent's face was pale as a sheet and he stood motionless for a long time before pulling the soaked map out of his t-shirt pocket.

Gilbert touched Trent's arm to get his attention and pointed back up the trail and then to his ear. Trent nodded and they walked up the trail until they could talk over the sound.

"Map shows a trail a few miles east that leads to an old logging road at the base of Gooseberry Mountain," Trent said with forced conviction. "It'll bring us out about ten miles east of our truck, but right on Route 28N in Newcomb, north of the Gooley Club. The worry though, is that we'll have to cross this same brook further up."

Gilbert looked back nervously. "Think we can?"

"We'll see."

"Don't have much choice, do we?"

"We don't have a lot of options. That is correct. But it's further up and maybe much narrower up there. At worst we should at least be able to lay a tree across and scooch over."

"Scooch over?"

"At worst," Trent assured and started folding up

the tattering map. "And let's switch these boots back. I got a good rest for my feet. Now you need one."

Trent's face didn't exactly match the supposed kindness of the gesture, but Gilbert agreed without feigning heroics and laced the boots onto his feet when Trent handed them over.

CHAPTER 12 | BACK

THEY RETRACED THEIR steps back to the junction where they had come out of the swamp earlier. Just beyond the junction was the river and another trail that went east up the river for a little bit and then turned back south in the direction they wanted to go.

At the junction, they turned onto the new trail, and about a mile up the trail, they heard the same dull roar as they had before, and they both knew. They checked anyway, and what they found was exactly what they feared. The torrent rushed through the forest at a width of at least twenty feet.

Trent held the map out, and he and Gilbert studied its deteriorating lines and graphics. The only option was a trail on the other side of Moose Creek. It would be a much longer hike, but all northern trails were 20 miles or more to a road, and they had already passed two of the three earlier and found them washed away at their inception by Cold River. That meant the bridge over Moose Creek and the trail after it was their only way out.

"Well, let's see if that bridge is still intact," Trent suggested.

"If not, we'll be completely trapped out here," Gilbert said, his growing despair thick in his voice.

They both heard rumbling somewhere, maybe in the distance, but neither could tell if it was Moose Creek telling them they were doomed, or thunder in the distance—or one of their stomachs.

CHAPTER 13 | BRIDGE

THE BRIDGE RATTLED and swayed and skipped off the surface of the river. It was being held by a single length of its wooden skeleton.

"We gotta get across!" Trent shouted over the roar. "It's about to go!"

"Wait!"

"We can't wait!"

Gilbert studied the map frantically. "How do we know the other rivers we'll have to cross on this trail won't be blocked? If we go over that bridge, we could be stranded even deeper into the woods than we are now."

"We've got to try."

Gilbert didn't know what to do. "At least on this side we're closer to the lake. Maybe we can make our way to the lake. Maybe we could find the canoe."

"You're dreaming, Gilbert," Trent shouted over the roar of the river. "We gotta go. We gotta *go!*" Trent turned and raced across the swaying bridge.

Gilbert watched him dart across and knew he now had no choice. He had to go where Trent went. They had to stick together. Regardless of anything else before or to come, that was their situation.

But as he stood there, the bridge shuddered and the wood creaked and the whole structure shifted three feet and dropped, wedged between the two abutments, pieces of the bridge snapping off and falling into the raging waters below. The one twisted piece of wood that held the whole bridge together was whining, screaming that it would let loose in seconds.

The fear of being alone in the woods overpowered the fear of the bridge collapsing, and Gilbert made a mad dash across. As his foot landed on the bridge, he heard the wood crack and felt the whole structure tremble and start to tip. Gilbert ran for his life as the supports heaved. He leapt off the bridge at the broken end and landed with a thump on the ground in front of Trent as the whole bridge toppled into the current and somersaulted downstream. From his stomach, Gilbert watched the bridge break apart until only a piece of its wooden framing remained intact, that piece settling into the rush of water and floating down the river with a splintered timber protruding up, like a broken mast on a sinking ship.

Trent wordlessly stepped over and helped Gilbert to his feet and pointed up the slope. Beneath a cluster of hemlocks, tucked away into the wind-whipped forest beside the now nonexistent bridge, an Adirondack lean-to rested on its sturdy timbers, awaiting weary travelers.

The sky was starting to darken and was made darker by the black storm clouds swirling overhead. They had to stop there. They estimated that they had done eight to ten miles of hiking and bushwhacking, alternating the one pair of boots between them. Gilbert hadn't walked eight miles in a row in his life, and certainly not through weather and terrain like they had faced today.

Now, there was no question about it: they had to rest and try to make it through the night. In the morning, they would try again. There would be no fire tonight, not in the rain, and there would be no food. Their packs and dry clothes were somewhere in Cold River, or on the bottom of Long Lake. They were soaking wet. But they had their sleeping bags in their mostly dry stuff-sacks.

They spent that night in discomfort, the pangs of hunger worse than the dampening sleeping bags.

But it would not compare with what was to come.

CHAPTER 14 | STARBURST

THE NEW DAY brought no let-up in the rain. Their muscles hurt, and their feet were swollen and cut and bloodied. Gilbert had developed a cough during the night and lay clenched in the fetal position inside his sleeping bag.

Morning only brought light, but no change in the chilling damp. The hunger pangs were now constant and unyielding. It had been thirty-something hours since they had eaten. They could think of nothing else.

"I want some candy so bad right now," Trent said, staring out the front of the lean-to, wrapped tightly in his sleeping bag. "I can't stand it."

"Oh man, and a can of soda," Gilbert said, from his bag.

"Fuck, that's so right! A can!"

Gilbert smiled. "Got to be a can. A can of Mountain Dew and a pile of Starbursts."

"With the wrapping already taken off of them. All pink!"

"No, no, no, no. Orange. A pile of orange Starbursts and a twelve-pack of ice-cold cans of Mountain Dew."

"Orange?" Trent said, surprised.

"Yeah," Gilbert said, smiling and nodding his head. "And a cheeseburger."

"Pancakes!"

"Ohhhh, covered in grade-A Adirondack maple syrup and cooked in butter so deep the edges crisp up and crunch, with gobs of butter melting over the top."

"Prime rib and buttery mashed potatoes."

"Oh, maaaaaan."

"Pizza."

"PIZZA!"

"Imagine if somebody delivered us a pizza right now," Trent said.

"Oh, my freaking goodness— Imagine if somebody just came walking out of the rain with a delivery bag full of Spring Street pizzas, piping hot."

They both looked out into the rain.

"What toppings do you want on yours?" Trent said after a minute.

"Just pepperoni."

"Of course just pepperoni, the king of toppings stands alone," Trent said, with what was becoming forced enthusiasm.

"Oh, man, could I go for a pepperoni pizza right now," Gilbert said, softer.

"And a bacon cheeseburger."

"Ribs."

"Joe's Kansas City."

They both sat silently smiling at the thought of food.

But there was no food. And their smiles along with their chuckling moods turned downward quickly.

For Gilbert, the anguish of the hunger came in the moments when it would leave his mind. Because then, when it came back, for just a moment he would get a very familiar feeling, a feeling of excitement he'd felt a million times before, when recognition of hunger had always led immediately to plans for what to eat and where. In his life before, that would be a joyous moment, because hunger made the idea of eating wonderful. It was those involuntary moments of joy that now spawned the worst moments of misery, the most agonizing of awakenings, the crushing re-alization that there was no meal to plan, no food to have—nothing to eat. It was completely foreign to him. The next meal had never been in question. There was always some-thing to eat. Something. Now, there was nothing.

Then, beside him Trent began stifling sobs. It was a terrifying sight. Trent, this strapping man, reduced to blubbering.

"Maybe we shouldn't talk about food anymore," Gilbert suggested.

Trent wiped his cheeks and laughed through a soggy mouth. "That's probably a good idea," he agreed.

Gilbert stretched his arms and yawned and scooted to the front of the lean-to. "What do you think?" he asked, looking out into the downpour.

"Well," Trent said and moved to the edge of the lean-to, "you ready to go out into it?"

"I guess."

"See if Calahan Brook is passable?"

"Let's hope to hell it is," Gilbert said and shook his head. "You think it is?"

"Let's hope."

It was nearly three miles to the crossing, and the going was rough. They rotated the boots every mile or so.

CHAPTER 15 | CROSS

IN FRONT OF Gilbert, Trent stopped and slumped to the ground as soon as they heard the familiar roar coming from Calahan Brook. Gilbert tried to get him up but he wouldn't move, didn't even acknowledge that Gilbert was there. He just sat and stared at the muddy ground.

It made Gilbert uneasy, terrified really, so he left Trent there to get his head right while he walked up to study the crossing.

The bridge was gone. He had expected that. But this brook was a little narrower than Pine Brook. Gilbert estimated that there was probably a similar amount of water traveling down the swath, but it was deeper and steeper, the water forced to move much faster and more violently, thundering to make the roar of Pine Brook seem like nothing.

The noise rattled in his brain, but he tried to stay focused. He moved upstream, looking for any way across.

Above him, the towering pine trees and tangled maple and birch wavered, their green limbs whipping sprays of water back and forth. The underbrush, weighted with rain, huddled nervously below the dueling elders. The wildlife was gone.

After some searching, Gilbert spotted a possibility. About a hundred yards upstream was an uprooted maple tree wedged behind two solid pines in the middle of the current. The underside of the tree was just into the water, but the torrent splashed and roiled over the top at times. It was treacherous, but if they could get to the trunk of the downed maple and across to the splay of muddy roots, they might be able to climb over and make a jump—a manageable jump—for the opposite bank. It was their only option.

But first, they would have to lay a log across to reach the top of the downed tree. This log only had to span about four feet of water, but that water was moving fast and was filled with stones and logs and anything else unlucky enough to find itself in that swath at that time.

Gilbert made his way down to where he left Trent and looked for a log to use along the way. When he reached the trail, Trent was standing with his hands on his hips studying the flow of water in front of him. When he saw Gilbert, he nodded and pointed back up the trail. Gilbert followed, and they walked until they could talk over the roar.

"I think I found a spot we might be able to cross," Gilbert shouted when they could talk. "There's a tree down that nearly spans the water."

"Nearly?"

"Well, we'll have to find a log to reach about four feet across. But it looks doable." Gilbert didn't mention anything about Trent's episode, and Trent offered no explanation.

Gilbert led the way up to the uprooted tree. Sapped by hunger, simple tasks like putting one foot in front of the other took massive energy to perform.

Along the way, Gilbert found a usable section of log, and they hefted it onto their shoulders and made their way to the crossing.

At the downed tree, Gilbert mimed his plan to lay the log across the open water to the trunk of the downed tree. Upon seeing the fast-moving current, Trent raised his eyebrows, but then nodded his head in reluctant agreement.

They stood the log on end and held it vertical. Gilbert moved behind it and lined himself up with the notch of a limb coming off the trunk. If he pushed it just right, it should land in the notch and rest securely with the limb on one side and the trunk on the other.

Trent held the log steady and pointed to the notch, silently confirming where the log should land. Gilbert nodded, then eyed it up one more time before giving the log a gentle but firm push. The log tipped slowly, like a felled tree, and then picked up speed before crashing down perfectly into the notch and settling against the trunk.

They both jumped as they saw it land, cheering into the roar. They stood for a moment, happy with their work, then wordlessly studied the route across, using hand signals to communicate.

Then, with a shrug of the shoulders that said they had no other choice, Trent stepped out onto the log and sprang across to the main tree before turning back to Gilbert and waving him across.

Gilbert steadied himself and took the first long step and caught a branch above him with his hand and guided himself into his second step. He flopped forward onto the trunk and flailed at the new limbs before finally catching one and steadying himself behind Trent.

Trent just shook his head with a slight grin and turned back to the main tree. Like a mountain lion, he scampered across in one fluid motion.

He reached the upturned ball of roots and turned and waved for Gilbert to follow.

This was a certified no-fall zone. One wrong step and it was *Goodnight, Irene.* Gilbert didn't know if he could do it. The water was so loud as he stood over it that it struck at his balance and made his knees wobble, upsetting his equilibrium. No matter how much he wanted to be anywhere but above that raging torrent on the trunk of a fallen tree, he couldn't make his legs move to take the steps necessary to get off of that log and across the water. He could see Trent shouting at him, but he couldn't hear what he was saying. He didn't have to. He was telling him to get the fuck on.

Gilbert took a deep breath, thinking, unhelpfully, that it could be his last. Then, with his breath held in fear, he leapt timidly and took three good, if wobbly steps across the log and one final not-so-good step that almost sent him to the current. But he kept his balance just enough and crashed into Trent and the ball of roots on the other side. He held himself there, clutching the wall of roots and looking down at the raging, frothing, brown water below the tree trunk he was standing on, trying to calm his racing heart and catch his breath.

The water was beginning to run behind the root ball on the other side, filling in the hole the tree had made when it upended. Across this, opposite the root ball, was a quickly eroding wall of earth that formerly surrounded and nourished the sturdy roots of the downed maple.

As they hung there, the dam of dirt beside the tangle of roots let loose with a sickening crash, and a violent pouring of water rushed in to fill the vacated space behind the upturned roots, cutting deeper into the opposite bank.

Gilbert and Trent could see their chances of crossing diminishing with every new inch the water cut into the bank.

Trent turned to Gilbert and motioned with his two fingers that they had to jump to the other side—

which was not good news for Gilbert. He was not an athlete, as was made clear in the canoe. But there was no choice. He could see Trent mouthing, "We gotta go!"

Trent climbed up onto the root ball and tossed his sleeping bag over to the other side, getting his feet set and bending his knees, gauging the jump. After that quick check, he motioned to Gilbert to hand up his sleeping bag and then tossed it over onto the other side with his, waving Gilbert up onto the root ball.

Gilbert started up, but Trent was in the way, so he motioned for Trent to jump first. Trent nodded and turned and took one deep breath then crouched to launch himself off the splay of roots. But just as he jumped, a four-foot block of sand and dirt and earth broke off the bank on the other side, disintegrating into the torrent. Gilbert saw it just as it happened. He saw Trent bend his knees to launch and at the same instant a thin crack suddenly appear on the bank Trent was leaping for, and the block of dirt move ever so slightly. Trent was just exploding out of his jumping motion when the whole thing let loose. He had no chance to stop himself.

But behind him, Gilbert lurched out and hooked his arm around Trent's right ankle and yanked Trent's foot into his chest and clutched it with all he had.

The ankle and elbow hooked, and Trent was jerked back in mid-air, swinging from the fulcrum of his ankle down with a crash, his head and shoulders splashing into the violent torrent of mud tearing down the mountain. But he didn't go in. Gilbert squeezed his foot to his chest and held on by sheer will.

Trent's head and shoulders bounced in and out of the water, and he flailed his arms trying to find something to grab to pull his face from the flow. He was being water-boarded by a flood. Gilbert could do nothing but hold on, and just that took every ounce of strength he had.

To make matters worse, the dirt had now completely washed away from around the roots of the tree and it was left suspended in the current, rocking with the violent flow assaulting the trunk and roots below the surface. The two trees the downed tree was lodged against held it steady in its position, for now, but the bottom of the downed trunk and roots were now bouncing violently in the flow.

Gilbert tried to look around to assess the situation, but he couldn't even turn his head for fear of dropping the ankle he held. He could do nothing but look up at the mountain and the deadly rush streaking down at them endlessly, and hold on. He felt Trent struggling but could barely see him. But then, out of the corner of his eye, he saw a flash, a hand, grabbing a root. Feeling the load lighten, Gilbert was able to turn to see another hand flash out and find a root and then Trent pulling himself and his head up out of the water with great effort.

Gilbert shifted with the change in weight and took the moment to strengthen his grip on Trent's leg. He dared to peek back down again, and he could see Trent's lips moving but the rush of the flood swallowed all sounds. There was only one thing to do: pull. Both Gilbert and Trent pulled with all their might and managed to get his waist over the top of the wall of roots and Gilbert then let his legs down and Trent hung over the roots on his stomach.

Trent hung there for a long minute and dropped his head and breathed a deep sigh of relief before eyeing the trunk of the tree behind him and lowering himself down to it with the guidance of Gilbert. His face and hair and whole top half were soaked in mud, and he was still emptying mud and water from his mouth, eyes, lungs, and sinuses, but he was alive.

The relief he and Gilbert felt was very short-lived. They were still on a precarious tree in the middle of a raging torrent.

At the other side of the flow, their log from the bank to the trunk still held steady in the notch of the limb, but the bank on the other end was eroding quickly. It was cut back to within two feet of the end of the log. They inched their way back.

At the other side, the four feet of water they had to cross on the log was now six. Which meant that instead of taking two steps with one foot placement to reach safely across, like they had on the way out, it would now take three steps and two careful foot placements out on the log, one of which wouldn't have a handhold above it. The difference was enormous.

When they reached the log, Trent bounced across in one fluid motion without stopping to think, making it safely beyond the eroding bank of the water.

Gilbert stopped to think. He had much less confidence in his ability to safely prance across a log with his life at stake.

On the bank, Trent frantically waved him across, shouting soundlessly into the roar.

CHAPTER 16 | LOSS

TRENT WALKED ALONG the trail and hung his head and squeezed the water out of the bottom of his shirt as if to keep from crying. He kicked his bare feet out in front of him with seemingly no regard for the cuts along his soles.

The rain was still pounding down and whipping around in the wind, and there was no end in sight. It was around noon, but the sky was as dark as dusk, made darker by the swirling canopy of the forest overhead.

Trent weaved down the trail, off-balance, with his chin stuck to his chest and his hands held limp at his sides. He was defeated, a pitiful sight of remorse and concession. He shook his head, and his shoulders slumped further toward the ground, and he suddenly crumpled into the mud and held his head in his hands.

Behind Trent, Gilbert looked on as a cold worry crept up his spine. Not the worry about their situation—which was dire. But worry about Trent. He was coming unglued.

"We'll be all right," Gilbert offered hesitantly, not wanting to further disturb the disturbed man. "We'll find a way out. Let's head back to the lean-to and figure out what we're going to do."

"I don't know what we're going to do," Trent whimpered as he stared off at nothing. He wasn't talking to Gilbert, or even himself.

"I know, man. We'll figure it out."

"I don't know what we're going to do."

"We're going to be okay."

"I don't know what we're going to do. I don't know what we're going to do. I don't know what we're going to do. I DON'T KNOW WHAT WE'RE GOING TO DO!" he screamed, and then screamed it over and over again as he shook his head and rocked back and forth and shivered with his arms clutched across his stomach.

Gilbert stepped back slowly from the outburst. He didn't know what to say or what to do, so he bent over, untied his boots, set them beside Trent and then walked back up the trail barefoot, toward the lean-to they'd seen at the trail junction a mile or so back.

He didn't look back but he could still hear Trent muttering and the sudden burst of screaming for the next few minutes until he was out of earshot into the woods. He walked through the pounding rain and assessed his situation. It was not good. But, for now, he just needed to make it back to the lean-to and get out of the rain.

The rain's relentlessness had begun to torture his

mind. The feel of the drip off of his nose drove him crazy. He tried to wipe it dry, for just one second, one second of pause in the incessant drip, and he wiped, and he wiped, but it was impossible, the stream kept coming and there was nothing he could do to stop it. It burned through his mind until he fully collapsed and covered his head with his arms. But even that didn't stop the rain.

CHAPTER 17 | FIRE

GILBERT SAT AT the edge of the lean-to and looked out into the downpour. He had taken his shirt off and was wringing it out, and he had dried his face with a rag left on a nail in the lean-to. Altogether, considering the situation, he felt okay. And despite soggy sweatpants, he was relatively dry from the waist up.

The lean-to he sat in was basically the same as the other two, but it was newer and had a fresh coat of paint and the logs were of a more uniform size and shape, having been milled with modern machines. The inside was larger than the other two, but it still had the same general size, shape, and look, with nails for hanging jackets and sweaters—which they didn't have—and a small shelf with a logbook and a few other things.

Gilbert rested his elbow on his knee and sighed deeply and looked out at the downpour. There hadn't been a let-up all day. It just kept coming and coming, raining and raining. He wrung out his shirt a few more times and then untwisted it and shook it out vigorously. There was no chance for a fire out in the rain, and making one under the roof of the lean-to would flood the shelter with smoke if he could even find wood dry enough to burn and something to start it with.

That thought made him remember the squares of fire-starters in the other lean-to. He slid his wet shirt on and stood up. The shirt was frigid cotton, but now only damp instead of soaking wet. He shivered as he stepped up into the lean-to and over to the shelf on the wall. The shelf held a broken spoon, a tin with a fishing lure and some line, a roll of aluminum foil, and a Dutch-oven pan with a latching lid. In a plastic baggie beside the pan was a pack of matches and the same fire-starters that they had seen in the other lean-to. There were three squares, and with shivering hands Gilbert quickly unwrapped them and broke off one of them. He took the aluminum foil from behind the Dutch oven and tore himself off a piece. He sat down in the lean-to and pulled out the matches and lit the corner of the fire-starter and held it upright until the flame engulfed it. Then he dropped it onto the piece of tinfoil on the floor and held his hands up to the tiny flame dancing off the little square of packed sawdust and petro-leum.

The warmth of the burning square was heaven on his fingertips. It spread from his fingertips to his hands to his arms and across his whole being. The fire-starter would burn for fifteen minutes or so, and he intended to make full use of that time. He lay down beside the flame and pulled his knees up until he nearly surrounded the flickering flame and it licked at his wet sweatpants. He held his hands on the far side until he made a full circle around the tiny fire and had drawn every part of himself as close as possible. It felt nice. It felt better than nice. It was heaven.

He reveled in the warmth and closed his eyes and his mind forgot about his aching hunger and he felt only the warmth, and the exhaustion. Any pains in his body and his muscles melted away as the warmth and darkness washed over him, and he drifted off into a deep and restless sleep.

Gilbert dreamed about poker while he slept on the floor of that lean-to. It was two years earlier, and he sat at the final table of the Turning Stone Casino Annual Potluck Poker Tournament. He was heads-up, one on one, against Benji Cheezle. Benji was something of a kid poker legend among the locals, and a common street punk besides.

"You're gonna check, just do it already," Benji sneered at Gilbert from across the felt. The full purse of American paper currency was piled on the table like a Mayan pyramid of cash and Benji grabbed a stack and started sniffing it with his eyes closed. The dealer relieved Benji of the stack with a chuckle and set it back amongst its brethren.

"Your play," the dealer said, still smiling as he pointed to Gilbert.

Gilbert stared at a bare circle of felt in front of him and ran the options in his brain. Cheezle was talking a lot. But he always did that. Gilbert still liked his three sevens, but there were three diamonds on the table. Benji had over-bet from the start. Was he chasing the flush? But the second and third diamonds had come on the turn and the river. Gilbert guessed Benji had an ace to match the one on the flop, and the slight rise over the customary doubling of his previous bet told Gilbert he'd paired up with the eight on the turn. Benji had been hoping for a boat on the river and was now feigning bravado because he was nervous about his two pair, and probably for the same reason Gilbert was nervous about his three sevens, because there were three diamonds on the table.

"All in," Gilbert said and pushed his stacks out into the open felt. He was short stacked to Benji by about two to one.

Benji leaned back in his chair and grinned at Gilbert. Gilbert sat with his elbows on the table and his arms crossed and stared out into the felt and thought about milkshakes and jelly beans and shaded beaches in Maine. As he sat and stared, trying not to move a muscle, his stomach tightened and he held himself still, the stomach muscles burning to keep his breathing steady. Benji studied him, and he began to sweat and wanted to rub the single droplet moving down his forehead, but didn't want to move. His stomach tightened and tightened and began to burn more with the effort. He could barely stand it.

And then the table suddenly felt red hot and his sweat sizzled off of it like it was a griddle, and before he could even think about that, the whole table burst into flames and began to burn and the cards and chips and cash caught fire and the dealer sat there as still as a monk, silently staring at Gilbert through the flames engulfing his body. Benji laughed a demonic roar and made fire shapes with the flames rising off of his hands. He got a kick out of it. But Gilbert just looked on in horror as the whole casino burned, smelling of charred flesh. He didn't understand. All the people in the casino, each a pyre of dancing flames, all stared at him, expressionless, the flames dancing and rising above them in twisting fire spouts. Benji was the only one with any expression on his face, and he was laughing. Gilbert looked down at his poker chips burning in the flames and saw that he, too, had caught fire. His stomach burned and he swatted at the flames, but they just grew larger and larger until he suddenly woke up in the lean-to with a crashing start, his shirt on fire from the fire-starter cube and the skin of his stomach burning. He flopped on his back and swatted at the flames and rolled over and back and forth on his belly until he smothered the fire into smoke.

When he rolled back over, there was still a sizzling hole the size of a grapefruit in his shirt and nearly all the hairs on his stomach within that circle were singed and he had a pinkish red open burn at the middle of the circle. It was a serious burn on his stomach, about the size of a fist, and it hurt like hell. Gilbert rolled on his back and writhed in pain, and the fire-starter cube still burned on the tin foil square at the front of the lean-to.

"Gilbert, your shirt is burned," he heard from the front of the lean-to. Trent just stood there at the edge of the torrential rain in his underwear. "What happened?" he asked.

"Oh, man, am I glad to see you," Gilbert said, truly glad, but still writhing around.

Trent nodded and looked down at the burning square of fire-starter. "Got too close, huh?"

"I did," Gilbert said and writhed.

"Get you bad?"

"Hurts like a mother," Gilbert said, and rose to his knees and arched his back and tried to air out and cool off his stomach.

Trent leaned over and looked at the burn on Gilbert's stomach. "Not too bad," he surmised. "Got you good, though."

"Yeah," Gilbert agreed and hopped on his knees and whistled his breaths as he stood up clumsily and hobbled out to the edge of the roof and stuck his belly out into the rain. "Ahhhhhhh," he moaned as the cold rain washed over the burn.

"Maybe you should see if anyone left some burn ointment or a med kit," Trent suggested as he wrung out his shirt and hung it from a nail.

"I didn't see any of that," Gilbert said. He smiled

in relief as he held his belly out into the rain. After a few long minutes of letting the cold rainwater run over his wound—and by doing so completely re-soaking any part of his pants or shirt that had dried—Gilbert turned around and stepped up into the lean-to. He inspected his burn and his shirt. The burn felt better, but it was still bad, an open burn. His shirt was in tatters and the whole belly was missing, and what was left was soaking wet and charred.

Trent looked up at him with drooping eyes. He looked like a child. Not in appearance, he looked ten years older and more grizzled in appearance, his normally carefully groomed look having deteriorated during their ordeal. And with his shirt off, being wrung out, he still showed the strong, muscular upper body of a fit man, ready to conquer any hurdle. But he looked like a child, *seemed* like a child. It was all in his eyes. They were terrified. Normally confident, even cocky, his eyes were now withdrawn and fidgety. He looked like a child that had peed his pants on the playground and was standing off to the side waiting in horror for the other kids to notice.

It made Gilbert uncomfortable. He looked down at Trent and started to speak, but then stopped himself and looked down again at his tattered shirt. "Burned my shirt," he stated.

"Yup," Trent said.

Gilbert tried to think of something else to say. For

a person who hated small talk, he now yearned for it. He opened his mouth to speak, but then still couldn't think of anything. With a shake of his head, he turned and stepped over to the shelf to look again for a med kit he knew wasn't there.

He moved the Dutch-oven pan on the shelf, and the aluminum foil and spoon and fishing tin behind it, but didn't find any med kit—as expected. He sighed and then stood there, staring at the shelf, trying not to think about the pain on his belly, squeezing his eyes open and closed as if that might help the pain go away.

One of these times, when he opened his eyes, he noticed the latch on the lid for the little nondescript Dutch-oven pan. His eyes narrowed and he put his finger under one of the latches and then flipped it up. Then the second one. He grabbed the lid and twisted it until the teeth lined up, then pulled it off the pan.

He almost didn't believe his eyes.

He stood there motionless for a long time.

Finally, he snapped out of it and slowly stuck his hand into the pot, touching the two bars, making sure they were real.

And then, without thinking, he covered them with his hand and scooped them out of the pot and slid them into his pants pocket.

He replaced the lid of the Dutch-oven, turning it fifteen degrees to tighten it down then folding the latches over each other, one by one, until the apparatus was returned to how he found it. Then he stood, staring at the wall behind the shelf.

"No med kit?" he suddenly heard from behind him. Too close behind him.

Gilbert snapped around and yanked the granola bars out of his pocket and blurted out, "I found these." He tried his best to smile and seem excited, as if he hadn't just pulled them out of his pocket.

Trent looked down and his eyes lit up at the sight of the food, and then turned darker than Gilbert had ever seen them. "Are those—?"

"Yeah."

Trent stepped closer, his eyes never leaving the granola bars.

Gilbert handed him one to stop his advance. "We're going to have to ration these," he said.

"Ration?"

"We don't know how long we're going to be out here."

"You can do what you want with yours, but I'm eating mine now."

"We really should ration them, shouldn't we?"

"Do whatever the fuck you want with yours," he yelled and tore into the package and took the bar out and threw the wrapper at Gilbert. He scurried to the front corner of the lean-to and devoured his bar with hunched shoulders and scouring eyes.

Gilbert watched Trent eating the whole granola

bar and shook his head. He took one of the corners of his and broke it off and placed it into his mouth. The lump of pressed flavors and sustenance rested on his tongue. It took a few seconds for his taste buds to reawaken, but when they did, it was like heaven. He moved the piece of honey-flavored bar around to all the corners of his mouth and let its sweetness melt all around his tongue. He closed his eyes and turned his face up to the heavens and let the food slide down his esophagus to the empty pit below.

When the first corner was gone, he paused and savored the flavor remnants in his mouth then popped another small bite into his mouth and repeated the whole process over again. When the second piece was con-sumed, Gilbert looked longingly at the remaining three-quarters of the granola bar, but quickly wrapped it up in the wrapper and jammed it into his pants pocket. He looked up at the roof of the lean-to and begged God to grant him the strength of will to not eat it immediately.

Before then, he'd never found much need to ask God for anything. His mother was quite religious and he went to church all throughout his childhood. But when he had prayed then, it was as a forced ritual that must be done to avoid a swat from his mother, and nothing more. He never had the feeling he was actually talking to any-body. Now, he hoped like never before that there really was somebody on the other end of the line, listening, hearing, able to help. He stared at the ceiling and took five deep breaths in succession, and with each one, he became more relaxed. He could still taste the flavor of oats and honey in his mouth, and that was enough.

When Gilbert dropped his eyes from the ceiling, Trent was staring at him, and a chill went down his spine.

But then Trent's eyes brightened and he smiled widely. "That was the most amazing thing ever," he proclaimed with a satisfied rub of his belly.

"Sure was," Gilbert said and rubbed the back of his neck, his eyes downcast.

Trent smiled. "Don't worry, Gilbert," he said with a chuckle, "I won't take any of yours."

"No, I wasn't—"

"It's okay, Gilly," Trent assured him. "I just do better if I get my calories right away. That was my share and I did what I wanted to do with it, and I won't even think about yours."

"Yeah, no, that's fine. It's not—" Gilbert stammered as he combed his hair forward with his palm.

Trent sat down on the edge of the lean-to and stretched his arms over his head and lay back with a satisfied smile on his face. "Man, what I wouldn't do for a cheeseburger right now," he said, staring up at the roof of the lean-to.

Gilbert didn't say anything.

"With crispy bacon and ketchup and mayo," Trent continued.

"I thought we weren't going to talk about food," Gilbert protested quietly.

"Ha," Trent grunted. "I guess we shouldn't, should we?"

They sat there in silence for a while, watching the rain.

CHAPTER 18 | CRAZED

GILBERT WOKE UP and immediately felt cold. Not only on the outside. An inner chill. His arms were crossed over the hole in his shirt and his boots covered his feet but did little to add warmth. When he opened his eyes, Trent was sitting at the edge of the lean-to, staring at him. Gilbert couldn't help but sit up with a start. His adrenaline pumped through his body, jolting muscles that were still sleeping. The effect was painful, and his heart pounded and ached. He couldn't calm his heart, but he tried to outwardly conceal his sudden fright. He made a show of stretching his arms and yawning, but never took his eyes off Trent, not needing to be a psychic to see the machinations taking shape behind his cold eyes. "How long have you been up?" he asked Trent as nonchalantly as he could, the real question within being *how long have you been watching me sleep?*

Trent turned away from him without expression and looked out at the rain that was still falling almost as hard as it had since it hit. "Not long," he replied. "How'd you sleep?"

"Good, I guess," Gilbert said and his heart slowly began to return to normal, though the shiver hadn't left his spine.

"I was thinking we should try some fishing," Trent said. "We've got that line and lure." He nodded to the shelf.

"Where?"

"The map shows a pond just east of here. There's probably fish in it."

"Okay," Gilbert said and stood up. "I'm gonna go take a leak."

Trent nodded his head and Gilbert stepped out the front of the lean-to and into the rain. He could feel Trent's eyes follow him as he stepped away. He could feel them burning through the pocket that held his granola bar. He skittered down the trail behind the lean-to, look-ing back often. His heart still hadn't slowed. He took deep breaths but couldn't quite catch it. He couldn't shake the chill.

He walked further up the trail, looking back, until he found a dense cluster of low-growing hemlocks that could serve as a blind. He ducked into the hollow in the middle of the hemlocks and peered through the branches back at the lean-to.

A few minutes later, he re-wrapped the granola bar carefully and placed it back in his pocket. The tiny morsel he allowed himself to consume had barely registered in his stomach. It took all his strength of will to not devour the rest. He took a deep breath and sighed. He was missing Jeannie terribly. What he wouldn't give to be lying in bed, under the warm covers and nestled against her plump backside. The thought brought a smile to his face, and then made him sadder than he had ever been in his life. He slumped down and sat for a long time with his back against the tree, looking out into that awful forest. He felt the tears well in his eyes and he fought them back with a grunt, scolding himself as he wiped his face and stood and stepped out of the hollow onto the trail.

As he stepped out of the hemlocks, he ran almost directly into Trent. Trent was just standing there in the rain. Gilbert jumped with fright and felt his knees turn to jelly and a whimper escape his lips. Trent didn't move or speak or change his expression. He just stood in the middle of the trail in the rain and stared at Gilbert.

Gilbert could hear the rattle of a squirrel out in the forest and a crackling of thunder gave warning from above. The rain had intensified again and was coming in sheets, nearly obscuring his vision of the lean-to.

"What's up?" was all Gilbert could manage to say. He knew Trent could see his fear. But Trent didn't seem offended. He seemed to almost relish it. *He's trying to frighten me*, Gilbert suddenly realized.

"Nothing," Trent replied without expression.

Gilbert eyed Trent warily and shifted his weight.

"You were gone a long time, and I got worried," Trent stated in a monotone.

"Oh," Gilbert murmured. "Thanks."

"No problem," Trent said with a smile.

Gilbert looked at Trent and subconsciously felt for the knife in his pocket. Trent didn't move and the rain poured down both of their faces.

"Wanna try fishing?" Gilbert asked, finally. "Like we talked about?"

"Sure," Trent said without expression.

"Okay."

"Okay."

The chill in Gilbert's spine was becoming a shiver and he pushed past Trent toward the lean-to just to keep his knees from buckling. He could feel Trent's eyes on his back as they walked up the trail.

Gilbert was practically scampering, but Trent stayed right behind him. Gilbert could hear Trent breathing. He felt a knot growing in his back, right between his shoulder blades, waiting for a sharp stick to come stabbing in. It was like when he was a kid and his older cousin would make him close his eyes and Gilbert knew a punch was coming, but he didn't know when or where. Sometimes his cousin would make him wait minutes before hitting him. The waiting was always worse than the punch. And now, he was waiting again—for something. He couldn't keep on. *Just do it already!* he pleaded internally. The knot was enveloping his whole back, and he writhed as he walked. Suddenly he stopped dead in his tracks and spun around on Trent.

Trent smiled at Gilbert when he spun around. He seemed to know exactly what Gilbert was thinking, and he seemed to love every second of it.

"What's up, Gilly," he asked with a smile.

I want to kill you! Gilbert screamed on the inside. *I want to take my fucking knife and drive it into your face!* But he just pressed his hair forward with the palm of his hand and said, "Do you want to lead?"

Trent chuckled at him as calmly and gently as if they were telling amusing stories over a glass of wine. "Sure, Gilly, follow me," he said and stepped past Gilbert.

Gilbert stalled on the trail and watched Trent move off in front of him. He looked down at his trembling hands then took a deep breath and palmed his hair forward. He couldn't take it anymore. But he took a few breaths and gathered himself and set out after Trent.

They grabbed the fishing line and lure from the shelf in the lean-to, and Trent led them up the trail with Gilbert struggling to keep up. They reached the pond after about a half-hour hike. Trent was standing with his hands on his hips surveying the body of water when Gilbert caught up to him. It was a beautiful pond, framed by the grade of the Santanoni mountain range, whose peaks were mostly veiled by a dancing mist—and the rain. The pond seemed very nice, but Gilbert didn't know whether it would have fish.

"Think there's fish in it?" he asked Trent.

Trent looked over at Gilbert, seemingly surprised at his arrival, almost as if he expected that he wouldn't follow. "Sure, it's got fish, Gilly," he said. "Just a matter of whether we can catch them."

Gilbert hated it when he called him Gilly, and it was really getting on his nerves that he kept doing it. He knew Trent knew it bothered him. But he also knew this was no time for pettiness.

"Well, all we can do is try," he said.

"Correct you are, Gilly," Trent replied with a grin.

Gilbert watched as Trent squatted down and pulled the fishing lure and line out of his pocket. He fed the line through the eye of the lure and twisted it, performed a fisherman's knot, pulling the line through itself and cutting the excess off with his teeth. He held up the lure and smiled at Gilbert. Gilbert tried to smile back.

"Think we'll get any?" Gilbert asked.

"I sure do," Trent stated.

The thought of food was intoxicating. Gilbert may not have been a big fan of fish before, but now a nice big fish sizzling over a fire sounded like heaven on earth. The thought gave him energy, made him forget his fear.

Trent made final preparation to the line and then set it down and clapped his hands together with a huge smile spreading across his face.

"We're gonna be eating like kings tonight, Gilly," he stated and blew into his fists.

Gilbert couldn't help but grin. He, too, rubbed his hands together in anticipation. Maybe they could get by until the storm cleared. Someone would definitely come looking for them, if they hadn't already.

"I'm thinking that over by that downed tree by the outlet is where the fish will be," Trent said and pointed. A quarter of the way around the pond, there was a large dead tree toppled over by the roots with its top in the water. It stuck out of the water right next to a stream outlet where the water was gushing out, charged by the rising waters from the storm.

"Okay," Gilbert replied with a shrug.

"Well, all right, then," Trent said. "Let's mosey on over and see if the fish are biting.

Gilbert nodded and they stepped through the wet forest, slowly making their way to the downed tree. The rain hadn't let up and just kept pounding down on them. Gilbert wasn't sure if it was better out in the open or under the canopy of the forest. In the open, it seemed colder, and steadier. But in the forest, it seemed to combine as it dripped off the trees to create huge splashing drops of rain. And the variation in the severity of the deluge only made things worse. It gave the slight sensation that it was letting up. Then with the next step they would walk under what seemed like an actual waterfall. The constant hope followed by dashing of hope worked to fray nerves that were already damaged.

Gilbert prayed to God to give them a fish. He

actually physically prayed. As Trent stepped off ahead of him, Gilbert stopped and dropped to his knees in the slushy mud and raised his eyes into the dropping rain and begged the Lord for fish. He didn't know what else to say while he prayed so he just asked for fish again and again, and then for someone to come help them, and then he crossed himself awkwardly and rose to his feet. Wiping the mud off his knees would be pointless, so he didn't.

At the downed tree, Trent was studying the surface of the water intently. Gilbert didn't know much about fish, but this seemed like a place fish would like. Trent didn't even seem to notice Gilbert as he stepped alongside him. Gilbert looked over at Trent and then down at the water and then back at Trent.

"What do you think?" he asked, just to say something.

Trent studied the water and didn't answer. So, Gilbert just looked down at the spot Trent was studying and crossed his arms. He really hoped there were some fish down there. His stomach was awakening with the thought of food and it began to ache again. It seemed that he could forget about his hunger for short periods of time. Very short periods. But even when he did, he could never really notice or enjoy the fact that he had forgotten his hunger because, of course, as soon as he realized he had forgotten his hunger, he remembered his hunger.

Presently, he was remembering his hunger painfully. He really wanted Trent to get the lure into the water so they could catch a fish. He didn't know what Trent was waiting for, and frankly, he didn't care. They wouldn't catch any fish with the lure out of the water. Of that much, he was certain.

"Whatcha doing?" he prodded.

"Just shut the fuck up, Gilbert!" Trent suddenly screamed at him, snapping around until his face was inches from Gilbert's. "Do you want to eat tonight or not?"

Gilbert jumped and stepped back. "Yeah," he stammered.

Trent glowered down at him. "Then shut the fuck up and let me think," he commanded and turned back to the water, muttering to himself.

Gilbert palmed the hair on his forehead and glared at the back of Trent's head. His heart was jolted with adrenaline from the unexpected outburst and he could feel the hair on his neck standing up. The hunger was getting to him. For a moment, he wanted to pound Trent with a tree branch. He actually wanted to see him bleed, to see blood coursing down the back of his head. He fantasized about it. He didn't know how long he stared at the back of Trent's head thinking about bloodying him, but, finally, he shook his head free of the image. He wanted a fish more. So, he took a few breaths and crossed his arms and stood behind Trent and let him think.

Finally, after what seemed like hours, but was probably only a minute or two, Trent stepped forward and tossed the line out into the water. Gilbert immediately forgot about his plans to pummel Trent's skull and instead stepped forward with an excited grin to watch the line. They were again on the same team. It was them against the fish, and the stakes were life and death.

Trent had tossed the lure right in between two of the branches from the downed tree. It was the perfect spot. Gilbert was so excited he couldn't stand still. He could taste the fish. He could feel it sliding down his esophagus, filling his belly. He rubbed his hands together in fixed anticipation and stared at the line for any movement. They both stared like that for what seemed like an eternity.

Then the line suddenly jumped and Gilbert jumped with it. His heart raced and his stomach dropped and he almost fainted right there on the spot. But it was just Trent taking in the line. Gilbert sighed and tried to keep his spirit from being crushed. It was just the first cast. The fish had to be down there. It was just the first cast.

Trent tossed the line back out. This time between two closer branches. Again, Gilbert stepped up and rubbed his hands together. Trent didn't even seem to notice Gilbert. He, too, just stared at the line.

After the first twenty minutes, Gilbert stepped back behind Trent and leaned against a tree. But every time Trent threw the line out, his heart still raced in anticipation. It went on like this for at least three hours.

Then it happened. It was on a cast like any other. Between the same two branches as his first cast, Trent gave the line a slight tug, about to bring it in, and the line went taut. He flinched and then froze with the line held in his fingers, and Gilbert jumped up from the tree he was leaning against, unable to stifle a yelp. He had been studying Trent and the line so closely that even this slightest variation of movement immediately keened his attention. He ran up beside Trent, and they both stared like madmen out at the line, trying to see the fish, to entice it to bite again.

Gilbert's eyes darted back and forth from where the line entered the water to Trent's hands holding it and back again. Trent calmly hushed Gilbert, never taking his eyes off the line. He held steady for three breaths and then the line twitched and he yanked it back to set the hook. Gilbert yelped and hopped and nearly fainted.

But then Trent dropped his hands, as if in defeat. Out of instinct, Gilbert lunged for the line that was now hanging slack in Trent's fingers. He looked at Trent in bewilderment.

"What are you doing?" he shouted, grabbing at the line. "Take it in!"

But Trent just stood there.

Gilbert snatched the line out of his hands. He didn't know what the hell was wrong with him, but if he wouldn't bring in the fish, Gilbert would. He took the line in his hands and started bringing it in. But it wouldn't come. And then he knew what Trent's problem was. But he didn't want to believe it. He pulled again and knew.

Gilbert slumped to the ground and sat in the mud

without care. He held the line up, handing it to Trent. Trent took it and sighed.

"Branch or a rock?" Gilbert asked.

Trent shrugged his shoulders and then stared up at the Santanoni mountain range across the water and sighed again. Gilbert hung his head between his knees and rubbed the back of his neck. He clenched his teeth and grimaced and slapped the mud in front of him. But then he took a deep determined breath and hopped to his feet and patted Trent on the shoulder.

"It's okay," he assured Trent. "We'll get it loose, and there are fish down there. We'll catch one."

Trent didn't respond, but he fixed his gaze back on the line and gave it a tug and tried to work it free.

It was ten minutes later that the line broke. When it did, Gilbert yelped like a kicked dog, and they both dropped to the ground. There would be no feast tonight, no fish at all.

"Give me some of that granola bar," Trent said.

Gilbert hesitated and his hand slid over his pants pocket. "But—" he started.

"Just give me a little," Trent demanded, rising to his feet over Gilbert. "Would you just let me starve to death?"

It was the first time death had been mentioned out loud, and the word hung in the air.

Gilbert reached slowly into his pocket and produced the granola bar.

CHAPTER 19 | SAVIOR

THAT NIGHT THEY spoke very little. Trent made a small fire under the eave of the lean-to with some damp twigs they had gathered on the walk back. But after only minutes, the fire had to be put out because it filled the lean-to with smoke. With no warmth and no fire, the two men sat silently on the floor at the open end of the structure, each within his own thoughts.

Eventually, Gilbert looked over at Trent. "I think I could find that lure," he said.

"How?"

"I'll dive down after it."

Trent just raised his eyebrows.

"We know right where it is."

Trent thought about it for a minute. "It's worth a shot," he said with a shrug.

Gilbert nodded and they became silent again and stared out opposite sides of the opening.

That night, Gilbert didn't sleep. He stared at the back of Trent's head the whole night.

*

THE NEXT MORNING found them back on the banks of the beaver pond. It was still raining. They were studying the water where the lure was hidden. Gilbert, stripped down to his boots and underwear, stood with his belly stuck out in front of him and his hair matted to his forehead.

"It was that limb there, right?" he said, pointing to one of the tree limbs in the water.

"I'm pretty sure."

"All right." Gilbert stood for a moment longer.

Trent looked over at Gilbert and chuckled. Gilbert was naked apart from his boxers and his boots, and he looked ridiculous, especially with the bright red burn on his otherwise milky white stomach.

"You ready?" Trent asked with a chuckle.

Gilbert grinned nervously as he looked down at the water.

"If you see any fish down there, grab them," Trent said with a smile.

Gilbert turned to Trent, at first thinking he was serious, and then smiled, nodding his head.

"Here goes," he said after a deep sigh, looking down at the water.

The short bank beside the downed tree was nearly vertical, so they moved fifteen feet down the shore to where there was a slightly more gradual access to the water. Gilbert sighed and took a step and slowly eased his way down to the edge of the water. After a slight pause he dropped one of his boots into the water and found footing on the soft, submerged slope of the pond. The bottom was steep, and with a tentative lunge he splashed out into the murky expanse and began treading water nervously, getting his bearings.

"How's the water, Gilbert?" Trent asked from the shore.

"Not bad, actually," Gilbert replied with a smile. And it wasn't. After being cold and wet for days, the water in the pond felt almost warm. Swimming with the boots on was a little awkward, but he was happy for the added protection, and, more importantly, the feeling of protection. Trent said there were snapping turtles in this area, and Gilbert didn't know if he was kidding or not.

Gilbert doggie paddled along the bank until he was in front of the limb they thought the lure was snagged on. Trent followed on the bank above him.

"This one, right?" Gilbert asked as he pointed to the limb.

"Yeah, I think."

"All right. Here goes." He took a big gulp of air and dove below the surface.

Opening his eyes, he grabbed at the thick tangle of branches and pulled himself deeper into the water, searching for the lure. Not finding it, he soon had to return to the surface for air.

"Didn't see it," he said as he emerged and shook the water off his head. "I'll take another look."

"I think it was about ten feet down," Trent said, pointing down into the water.

Gilbert dove again and didn't see it. And again, and again.

For nearly an hour, he dove over and over, searching for the lure, but found nothing. His lips had turned a ghastly shade of blue, and he was shivering terribly, but he kept diving.

Trent watched from the shore, showing more and more annoyance each time Gilbert rose without the lure.

Gilbert came up from one dive and hung from a branch above the water, breathing deeply. He and Trent hadn't spoken for the last half-hour. There wasn't much to say. Gilbert just stared at the rock and mud of the nearly vertical bank in front of him and tried to catch his breath, and Trent stared down at the water.

Gilbert breathed in and out a few times fast, then took a deep breath and held it and dropped down below the surface. Under the water, he waited for his eyes to adjust to the murky water and then pulled himself down into the tangle of the tree. There was a small, dark, recess in a deep cluster of branches that was still unchecked. He swam and pulled himself down toward it, nearly fifteen feet below. His ears pounded with the pressure and he tried to control his exhaling to best preserve his oxygen.

As he approached the recess, he saw something

inside. A flash of color. He dove closer and cranked his neck and adjusted his body to see inside. He pulled himself down by the other branches and held his breath fully so the bubbles wouldn't obstruct his view. The recess was very dark, but he could see something in it. He drew closer, and the object moved and flashed a dull orange for a moment and then disappeared again.

Gilbert pulled closer and closer and felt his lungs fighting to breathe. He reached the recess and stuck his hand down into the darkness hoping to find the lure waiting inside. He felt his finger brush against something. He reached and snatched at the object and yanked it out of the recess. He looked down through the murky water at a small, orange, maple leaf floating in his hand.

He yelled into the water and threw the leaf aside. He punched out at the empty water in frustration as he reoriented himself vertical and kicked toward the surface. But as he started to the surface, he suddenly felt a searing hot sharpness on the back of his calf. He flailed and looked down through the water and saw the unmistakable brown outline of a beaver dart away though the murky water. A bloody flap of skin hung from the back of his calf and a trail of crimson wafted through the water. He screamed again in horror, and flailed for the surface. With every move, he thought he saw the outline of the beaver returning, the razor-sharp teeth ready to strike.

Gilbert's lungs were burning, and he kicked for the surface and his arms darted out into the air. But just as his head was about to break the surface, his upward motion stopped dead as something grabbed his foot. He flailed to try to breathe, but his lips would go no further than six inches from the surface. What had him? The beaver? He thrashed and lurched and tried to break free. But to no avail. He kicked for the surface, but couldn't kick his one foot, and couldn't get his lips to air.

He looked back down at his foot and saw only black water. He yanked and nothing happened. He panicked and wanted to breathe. Then finally, he saw that his bootlace had become ensnared on one of the branches of the sunken tree. He kicked to get it free, but it wouldn't budge. He looked up out of the water and thrust his hands up to Trent, who stood on the bank of the pond, directly above him, motionless, looking down at him.

Gilbert screamed from underwater with the last of his air and reached his hands desperately to Trent, only his hands and wrists breaking above the surface.

But Trent just stared down at him and watched.

Gilbert thrashed and flailed, reaching for Trent. And when Trent didn't help, Gilbert's lungs, unable to be put off any longer, drew in the cold, murky water. The water drove into his lungs like a thousand tiny knives, and he watched through the rippling surface as Trent stood motionless.

CHAPTER 20 | LOVE

"Do we even know what Trent does?" Jeannie asked as they sat at their house, two months before the canoe trip, cozying in on a rainy Sunday afternoon. It was early summer, and the windows were open, despite the rain. They had hardly moved all day. Gilbert had cooked up a breakfast of bacon and eggs and French toast, and they ate and drank coffee and watched the warm, summer rain dripping off the eaves outside the window.

After some lazing and puttering about in the morning, Jeannie had brought out some warmed apple cider and dice, and they were playing Shoot the Moon for chores. Jeannie would do most of the chores anyway, and redo anything Gilbert had done, but Gilbert knew she just liked to bet on something. He often laughed when she got locked into a bet or a line of wager at one thing or another. She was a fiend. It was why she was a pediatric nurse and he was a poker player. But at home, for a dollar, or a backrub, or sweeping out the garage, she loved to gamble.

Nobody else that knew her would have ever guessed. She appeared as wholesome as a baby calf to most people she knew. But Gilbert got a kick out of some of her less-wholesome traits.

"I think he said he does something in trucking or excavation or something," Gilbert answered. "I asked him once and he was vague about it, and I haven't really talked about it since."

"Hmmm," Jeannie said as she poked and prodded the knick-knacks and ticket stubs in the catch-all cigar box she'd found the dice in earlier—now sitting on the dining room table beside them. She was leaned over the small case as if it held all the answers in the world. Garbage, mostly, from one adventure or another. She was curious, though, and Gilbert loved her for it.

"Has he been good to Liz?" Gilbert asked, leaning back in his chair.

"I guess."

Gilbert picked up the dice and shook them. "So, it doesn't matter then?"

"I know," Jeannie said, raising her palms up and turning to Gilbert, shrugging, unable to let it go. "I just know Liz, and she's not always the smartest about who she chooses to fall in love with. And once she's in love, she doesn't pay a damn bit of attention."

Gilbert kept his mouth shut. He knew it was fine for her to say anything she wanted about her sister, but not anybody else, even Gilbert.

"Don't just sit there mute," she said, waving her hand. "You can say what you want."

"No, nothing," he said, getting up from the table and moving into the living room, sitting down in his reclining chair. "I know you're worried, like always, but I'm sure she's fine," he said as he sat down. "Really. Trent seems like a good enough guy. He's kind of macho, but he seems okay."

"I know," she said, resting her chin on her hand on the table.

"You worried about something specific?"

"No. Not at all."

"No?" Gilbert said, grinning.

"I'm just overly protective."

"No way," Gilbert said, grinning wider.

She shooed him with her fingers and looked out the window. "What does it matter what exactly he does for a living anyway? She says he has work, and he's covering most of their bills."

Gilbert rolled his eyes, playfully. "Maybe he's in the CIA. Maybe he sells women's underwear. It's not really our business."

"You're no fun, Gubby," she said and smiled, moving over to Gilbert's chair and laying down on top of him, the old leather reclining chair creaking under their notable combined weight.

He smiled up at her and they kissed.

"How did I get so lucky," he said, looking into her eyes.

"You haven't gotten lucky yet," Jeannie said with a sly grin.

"Yet?" Gilbert said.

"Yet," Jeannie said and kissed him on the lips.

CHAPTER 21 | SUNK

As GILBERT'S LUNGS drew in pond water, he thought of Jeannie and fought for all he was worth in one final effort to survive. He lurched for air, but he hung at that same spot, six inches from the surface.

He kicked and kicked, and from below, he heard a muffled, sharp snap, and his foot suddenly came free. He kicked once more and his head burst above the surface and he coughed out the water in his lungs and gulped for air. As his head reached above the surface onto the muddy bank, Trent squatted down, in no rush, and grabbed his arm and pulled him up onto the grass.

Back on solid ground, Gilbert coughed and spat and scampered backwards across the ground like a crab, pressing his back against a tree, staring at Trent in terror.

"What the fuck was that?" he shrieked between gulps for air.

"What was what?" Trent responded calmly.

"What was *that?*" Gilbert yelled, pointing to the water. "I almost drowned and you just watched!"

"Oh," Trent said calmly. "I had no idea you were in trouble."

"Bullshit you didn't," Gilbert shrieked, still coughing and gasping for air. His leg was bleeding badly where the beaver had bitten him.

Trent just stared out over the water with his back to Gilbert.

"Did you get it?" he said after a long pause.

"Did I get it?" Gilbert parroted.

"Yes. Did you get it?"

"Did I get *what?*" Gilbert asked.

"Did you get the lure, Gilbert. The thing you went in the water for. Did you get it?"

"No, I didn't fucking get it, Trent!" Gilbert yelped.

"I didn't think so," Trent said and looked down at his hands, his back still to Gilbert. He used a thumbnail to scratch at a callus on his palm, and he sighed deeply. "I didn't think so."

Gilbert had regained his breath and was staring at the back of Trent as Trent turned around. Gilbert followed his eyes down to where Gilbert's pants were piled on the ground. The last piece of granola bar was in the pocket—and his knife.

When Gilbert looked back up at Trent, Trent was staring straight at him. Gilbert jumped to his feet and scurried over to his pants and shirt. He snatched up the clothing and pulled the partially burned shirt over his head and clutched the pants tightly to his chest.

Trent watched Gilbert without moving. As Gilbert clung to the pants, their eyes met. Trent took a step closer to Gilbert and Gilbert took a step back.

"What do you say you give me those pants and that last piece of granola bar?" Trent said calmly.

"No way in hell," Gilbert said.

Trent locked eyes with Gilbert.

"You're not getting them," Gilbert said with as much bravado as he could muster, fumbling the pants around and around to find the pocket with the knife.

"Yes, I am, Gilly."

"Stop calling me Gilly."

"Gilly, I'm gonna have those pants and that bar," Trent said and produced the knife Gilbert was looking for, unfolding it slowly.

Gilbert took a step back at the sight of the blade. "How did you—?" he said, grabbing at his pants pocket where the knife had been.

Trent calmly looked down at his hands and used the tip of his blade to clean out a fingernail. "I said, I'm gonna have those pants and that bar."

"What, so you're gonna kill me over a half of a granola bar?" Gilbert spouted, shaking his head. "Or do you want to say what this really is?"

Trent squinted his eyes and looked down at Gilbert's boots. "And I'll take those boots, too, Gilly," he said, "while we're at it."

Gilbert stood with his mouth open. Trent's eyes

moved up to his and locked, deadpan. Gilbert looked back and forth at the forest around them.

"You know I can outrun you," Trent said, reading his mind. He took a step closer and pointed the knife. "Especially with that nasty gash on your leg."

Gilbert looked down at the bite on the back of his calf.

"Hand them over, Gilly," Trent said.

In a split second, Gilbert made a decision. He turned and ran, darting behind a tree to get around Trent.

It was a noble idea. But before he could take more than two steps, Trent sprang like a cat and emerged on the other side of the tree. With an expert lunge and a thrust of the blade, he drove the knife deep into Gilbert's side. Gilbert went to the ground with a squeal. He rolled over onto his back and clutched his hands over the knife-wound in his side, watching the deep crimson liquid seep out between his fingers.

"You stabbed me," he whispered.

Trent reached down and picked Gilbert's pants up off the ground and stood up. "Now the boots," he said.

"You stabbed me," Gilbert repeated, still staring down at the blood and the wound in his side.

Trent held the knife in his right hand and reached down with his left and untied Gilbert's boots and pulled them off his feet.

CHAPTER 22 | WOUNDS

GILBERT WOKE UP freezing cold. He was in the same place Trent had left him. It was still raining. His legs were bare up until his underwear, and his shirt was half burned. Blood stained his boxers and the bottom half of his shirt, and there was a large gash in the now-red cotton where the knife had gone through. A trail of blood ran down from that wound onto his boxers, and another trail ran from the wound on his left calf and over his bare foot. He moaned as all the pain hit him at once.

Gilbert looked up at the sky because he couldn't bring himself to look at his wounds. Slowly, he rolled himself over until he was on his back, his head resting on the muddy ground. The rain pounded down on his head and a throbbing headache grew worse with the movement, every thick drop of rain feeling like a strike from a hammer. He was thirsty, and he let the rain drops fall onto his extended tongue. He lay that way for a long time, the relentless rain washing over him.

Eventually he rose to his knees and crawled through the mud. He could still see the boot prints Trent made when he left. Holding the wound in his side with one hand, Gilbert dragged himself slowly down the trail toward the lean-to, following the boot prints. When he reached the lean-to, it was empty.

He crawled under the eave and stopped to rest before pulling himself up onto the floor. Once on the wooden planking of the lean-to, he rolled onto his back and lay there, reveling in the cover from the rain.

He curled himself up and slid in and out of consciousness and fitful dreams. In his dream, he was at the final table again. But this time, all the players were the Bogacci Family mobsters from his game at the Sacrament Marina on Lake George. The setting changed, as it does in dreams, from the casino, to the back bar at the Sacrament Marina, to there, inside the lean-to. This time all the hardened killers were staring at him wordlessly across the lean-to. He held triple sevens again, and they stared and stared with cold faces, and then their faces began to grow and grin, and they grew and grew, up over him, their grinning snarling faces salivating at his fear while turning into maniacal smiles that filled the tiny woodland structure. Jimmy Dove started laughing first, a rolling, grinning chuckle that grew from the first moments into a booming roar that all the other killers joined in on, laughing and laughing and laughing at the tiny pitiful nothing whimpering in front of them.

"He just takes it like a nobody," the boss, Salvo Bogacci, laughed, nudging his *consigliere* in the ribs. "Look at how his friend just stabs him and robs him and he just takes it. Give me your chips, you little shit," he said, reaching over and grabbing Gilbert's remaining stacks of chips from the poker table between them. "Yours are mines."

Gilbert awakened from the dream and the pain flashed throughout his body. He was lying on his side, curled into a ball. He shook his head clear and looked out at the rain. He closed his eyes and laid his head back down on the wooden floor. The wind blew the rain into the lean-to, and he was wet.

After a long time, and with a deep sigh to steady himself, he opened his eyes and quickly stole a peek at the knife wound on his side and then closed his eyes again. Seeing the wound made it hurt like hell. And it was ugly. He stole another glance and then squeezed his eyes shut. It was bad.

He squeezed his eyes harder and tried to sleep. He just wanted to sleep. He wanted it all to go away. He shivered in the cold and squeezed his eyes closed and tried to will himself to sleep. But it was pointless, and soon, tears started to stream out of his closed eyes, and he shook and clutched himself and cried. He missed Jeannie. He could see her face laughing across the breakfast table. She was his beauty. Her cheeks were full and made her smile warm and contagious. Gilbert thought she was perfect. She was the most beautiful thing in the world to Gilbert. She caused the sun to shine.

Gilbert wiped the tears away from his face and made himself look down at his wounds. They needed to be treated, somehow. He would die of blood loss—or something—before long.

"Okay, you can do this," he assured himself, speaking out loud. The sound of his own voice in the hollow of the empty lean-to made him feel very alone, but also reminded him that he was still alive, that he could still make sound, make noise, breathe, and put words out into the world.

He used his elbow to push himself up and swung his legs in front of him, sitting at the edge of the lean-to. The movement made him dizzy, and he took a long moment to recover his balance and vision.

The rain poured down outside. Gilbert steadied himself and pulled off his burned shirt. He looked down at the wound, still seeping blood. He took a deep breath and stood up slowly, to not lose consciousness. He staggered out into the rain and slumped down on a log beside the soaking wet fire pit. The center of the pit was a deep puddle of ashy water and Gilbert stared down into it as he gathered his strength.

First, he arranged himself so that both wounds pointed up toward the rain. He stayed that way for a long time and let the pounding rain cleanse his wounds. Next, he scooped some wet charcoal from the bottom of the fire pit and smeared it over the wounds. He'd seen that in a movie, he thought, and it was all he could think of. Then he cleaned his shirt in the rain, scrubbing, rinsing and wringing it out over and over. When satisfied, he moved back into the lean-to and ripped the shirt into two pieces. He used one piece to wrap around his mid-section, over the wound in his side. He pulled it as tight as he could and tied it off. He did the same around the wound on his leg with the other piece of the shirt. And then he was shirt-less, but bandaged.

CHAPTER 23 | CHOICE

T RENT HAD TAKEN everything of use from the lean-to. He left the bent spoon, the pan and the journal, but most importantly, the fire-starters and matches were gone, as was the map.

Gilbert tried to remember the features of the map. Long Lake ran north-northeast, and Gilbert was east of the north end of the lake, near Moose Creek. He knew that the direct route back to the road was cut by creeks and streams that would be the same as the other creeks they had found. He looked out of the lean-to at the Santanoni mountain range. The only way around the water was to get above it, where the streams hadn't become torrents yet, like the winter snowshoers in the journal. Gilbert and Trent had discussed it as a last case scenario the night before: to go along the ridgeline of the Santanoni range. He concentrated, trying to remember the map. The mountains were in something of a horseshoe, and if he could reach the western ridge, he could follow it around and eventually south, almost to the road, while staying above any swollen creeks.

Gilbert thought of Trent and looked down at his side. The dressing showed red over the wound and gray from the charcoal. He stared at the spot for a long time, stroking his hair forward with the palm of his hand. Eventually, he grew very weary and moved to the back corner of the lean-to and curled into a ball and fell asleep.

When he awoke, it was night. He was shivering. The forest was a blur through the rain. He sat up and pushed his back against the rear wall of the lean-to and watched the rain fall in the blackened forest.

Listening to the rain driving into the roof and watching the streams cascade off the eave, he drifted into a daze and stopped thinking altogether. His mind receded into emptiness, and with it, went the pain and the cold and the hunger. A warmth returned and comfort percolated up through him and his mouth lay open and he closed his eyes and his head rocked forward and he fell asleep—or passed out.

The sky was a lighter shade of gray when he awoke. He rubbed his eyes and stretched his aching neck and guessed that it was just after sunrise. His body hurt all over, and his stomach was torn with hunger. He felt like it was sucking the rest of him into it. His cheeks were hollowed by its pull and the bags under his eyes felt like they were slowly melting away from his face. Moving in any way seemed impossible. Even the groan he was emitting took great effort—but it was his only form of release. Nothing made anything feel better.

He shivered in the cold, and every muscle ached with the effort of shivering. He knew that if he were to leave the lean-to and try to travel the ridge of the Santanoni range in his current state, he would die. But he didn't know what to do instead.

He curled himself around himself as best he could and shivered. Was any rescue coming? What should he do? He shivered until he fell asleep again.

He awoke with a start and realized he was dying. It was afternoon, as best he could tell, and the rain had slowed slightly. He could feel the sun setting on his life, like it would soon set on that day behind the wall of clouds that obscured it. This would be his final sunset, he realized, and he wouldn't see it. He would die right there without even making a run for it.

A run for it was suicide.

He tried to make himself concentrate.

He would die trying, he decided. He had to at least do that—for Jeannie.

He thought for a long time. There had to be a solution. He needed some kind of clothing, something to cover his body, to keep the rain off and to retain a little warmth. He was already weak from his wounds and lack of food. He knew his chances were non-existent without some kind of protection from exposure, and the same without food.

Without shoes or a map, he estimated that it would take him four days and three nights to traverse the range and arrive at the road. He would need some kind of shelter each night. His feet were already bloody and cut. He would need something to act as shoes.

His mind worked through a list of what he would need and how he could obtain it. He tapped at the lean-to floor with his fingertips and stroked his chin. Putting together a list made him feel better. It occupied his mind. It gave him something to work toward.

He stood up slowly in the lean-to, controlling his dizziness, and stumbled to the shelf. The first thing he grabbed was the Dutch-oven pan. He opened it and placed the pan under the eave and it was soon filled with water. He took a long drink of the water and it was delicious. Despite being in a torrential downpour for days, he had failed to keep himself hydrated, and the water was much needed. He set the pan aside and stepped up to the shelf.

There wasn't much. Apart from the pan, all that Trent had left was the bent spoon and the journal—which was inside a plastic Ziploc freezer bag with a pencil.

He sat and frowned and shivered in the cold. He tried to clear his foggy mind. He tried to think. What could he use for clothing?

He looked around the lean-to. It was bare. Logs and planks. The rain pounded down on the roof. What could he even use? If he tried to hike that far in this weather shoeless and naked, he was as good as dead. He needed something.

He looked around the lean-to again—and it was still bare.

But a tiny puddle in the back corner of the lean-to gave him an idea.

Every two or three seconds, a drip came down from the sloping rafter beam above. He went to the corner and watched the drip, once— twice— three drips. He leaned forward and looked at it closely. It was dripping off a splinter in the wood, cause by a knot in the thick timber. The water was dripping down from that knot, but it ran there from above. He followed the stream up its course, and it came from a seam in the wood roof and then ran over to the beam and along its side for a foot or so before diverting down the beam and eventually to the knot. Gilbert sat and stared at the water for a long minute, touching the drip with his finger and watching it form another perfect droplet the moment he pulled his hand away. It would hang, as if struggling to break free, and then in a heart-dropping, shuddering instant, it would break loose, rebounding and bouncing in a pulsating free-fall toward the floor and the puddle below.

He wiped the knot one last time and then stepped out to the edge of the lean-to and up to the wall of rain. He stood there as if the rain might stop altogether for just a moment, just while he checked what he had to check. But it didn't. Though lightening, it dropped now in a taunting monotone. Gilbert fought the growing frustration, the growing rage. *Just stop, damn you!* But the sky hung above and paid no mind to Gilbert Willards below. The sky did not know what or who Gilbert was. Didn't care. It only rained and blew wind. It only moved over, and past, and yet stood in every direction at all times.

Gilbert looked up at the sky, but he only saw the rain, and with the sour venom of powerlessness to stop what he wanted to stop coursing through his weakened veins, he stepped out into it. Outside he moved around the back of the lean-to and found what he was hoping for. Shingles on the roof. He inspected the roof and found a loose shingle and pulled it off, exposing the tarpaper below it. He and Jeannie had had their roof replaced two years before, and how he'd come to hate those devil ingredients: tarpaper, nails, and shingles. They ended up in all of his flower gardens and in his lawn, often with nails still embedded in the shingle and pointing to the sky, waiting for a bare foot to find its mark. He found remnants in his bushes for three months after replacing his roof, but right now, he'd never been so happy to see anything in his life.

He grabbed a bent stick to help and shimmied himself up onto the low back eave of the lean-to. He got to his knees and found his balance on the roof, then made his way to the peak and started prying off shingles with the stick, careful to pull the nails with the singles. In an hour, he had a whole pile of shingles beside the lean-to and he had uncovered and cleared a ten-by-ten-foot section of roof. Starting on the edge, he carefully peeled back the tarpaper at its seam, popping its staples and rolling it back until he reached the edge of his opening, where he tore it off. After one strip, he had a three-foot by ten-foot section of fairly intact tarpaper.

An hour later, he was inside the lean-to with four rolls of tarpaper and a pile of shingles. With a deep breath, he slowly untied his bandages. He only allowed himself the slightest look at each of his wounds. There was nothing he could do right now anyway, so he looked quickly and then moved on. He ripped as many small strips of cloth as he could spare from what was once his shirt, and then he redressed his wounds with the makeshift bandages and lay back against the wall of the lean-to. With his remodel to the roof, the lean-to was now only half-functional. The side he sat on was nice and dry, but the side over which he had removed the roof was now leaking, droplets streaming down from the nail holes, onto the planks, and out the corner of the lean-to.

Then he set to work.

CHAPTER 24 | CREATION

By NIGHTFALL, GILBERT had cut the tarpaper into pieces using a sharp rock. One piece was about five feet long and three feet wide, tapering in on the ends. He cut a hole in the middle for his head, and the other two sides he folded down and tied around his waist to make a primitive shirt or vest. From another piece he cut long strips that he layered and strung together with the cloth so they'd hang around his waist and make something of a skirt.

Using the pages from the journal and the plastic from the Ziploc bag it was in, he stuffed the crumpled paper inside the tarpaper to act as insulation and padding, and he used the plastic to line hot-spots where the tarpaper rubbed against his skin, like around his neck where he'd fashioned himself a plastic and paper collar to make the neck hole a little more comfortable, almost like a Renaissance painter, he thought—or the Joker in a deck of cards—or a man about to die in the wild.

With the shirt and skirt made, he cut two shingles

in the outline of his feet, and with cloth thongs, made himself something resembling a sandal. With another piece of tarpaper, he cut a circle, and then a radial slit from the center to the outside. After overlapping it over itself and then fastening it with the cloth under his chin, he ended up with a pretty damn good conical hat.

He smiled at all of his creations, and then put them on and tested his new ensemble out in the rain. It worked pretty well, considering.

"I head out at first light," he said to himself as he stepped back under the eave. He had started talking to himself. The sound grounded him, made him know the deteriorating connection he had to the real world didn't mean it wasn't there.

He breathed deeply and sighed, daunted by the task these makeshift clothes represented. He pulled off the hat and twisted to get a better angle at the strap on the side of his tarpaper vest to release it. But as he turned, he howled in pain and dropped to his knees. The pain came in a rush, not a flash, but a rapidly growing, searing hot pain. He stopped twisting the second he felt the first pangs of discomfort, but by then, it was too late. The pain rushed into his side and sent him to the ground. He whimpered and dragged himself around, as if the movement would help, as if he could scramble away from the pain like it was a wasp. But nothing slowed the slicing agony once it was set on its course.

Eventually, it crested and subsided enough that he

could pull himself up into the lean-to. In the moments when the pain went away, he was the most comfortable he'd ever been in his life. The stark contrast, the juxtaposition of white-hot pain with nothing, combined with his exhaustion and loss of blood, made the moments between the waves of pain almost feel angelic, a nap on the most calming, soft sand beach. But then the pain would come back like a Nazi blitz flashing through the night, breathing death and chaos. It carried on like this, and with time and repetition, it wore on his mind, and it exhausted his body, and in time, the exhaustion beat the pain, and he fell into an uncomfortable and restless sleep.

CHAPTER 25 | BUCK

IN A FLASH of lightning late that night, Gilbert first saw
Buck. He had slept for a few hours, but awoke freezing
and damp. It was raining hard again and his cough now
felt raw with sickness. He was clenching his teeth against
the cold and staring at the wall of water coming off the
roof when he spotted a person out of the corner of his
eye. First, it was just a shape in a lightning strike, walking
along the tree line out in the rain. Before Gilbert could sit
up, it disappeared into the forest.

Gilbert sat silently for a long time, staring out
where the figure disappeared. Then a series of flickering
lightning strikes revealed the man out in the forest again,
moving to the left along the tree line, eventually cutting
out of sight behind the wall of the lean-to.

In the last strike, Gilbert could see him clearly. He
was a tall man in a black wide-brimmed hat and a black
rain slicker that ran down to his boots. The man never
looked over at Gilbert or the lean-to.

Gilbert shifted to try to get a look around the wall of the lean-to.

"Hello," he croaked, holding his side where the knife wound bled through the bandage. No response. "Hey— mister," he tried to yell.

There was no sign of the stranger for a long, tense series of anticipatory moments.

"Hello?" Gilbert yelped again, slumping toward the front of the lean-to. He was sure he had seen him. He had seen something. He took two long deep breaths and gathered his strength. There was a sudden energy that coursed through him that came with a renewed will to go forward, to stand up, to get the attention of the man he just saw.

He shook his head and stood up—cracking his head viciously on the angled cross-timber of the low lean-to roof. The blow sent him back to his knees, stars exploding out of the corner of his vision. He rested on one knee and held his head. Then he heard something move through the brush behind the lean-to, snapping twigs.

"Hello," he croaked. "Mister." But there was no reply.

Gilbert rose to his feet again, bending to avoid the timber this time, and then shuffled to the front of the lean-to and around the corner.

As he hit the cold rain of the lean-to's edge, he came face to face with a giant, grizzled man.

"You don't look so good, bub," the man said, looking down at Gilbert.

Gilbert almost fell over from the surprise. "What are you doing out here?" Gilbert asked, trying to shake the cobwebs from his head.

"What am *I* doing out here?" the man parroted. "What are *you* doing out here?"

"My friend and I got caught in the storm."

The man almost looked like an old Western gunslinger as he stood there. "Where's your friend?" the gunslinger asked.

"I don't know," Gilbert said, shaking his head, confused. "I guess he's not my friend. Can you help me? Are you a park ranger or something?"

"Sure, I can help you."

"Do you have any food?"

"I'm afraid I'm in the same boat as you, as far as food goes."

"Do you have a way out of here?"

"Same way as yours, right over those mountains." He pointed into the black rainy night in the direction a mountain range might wait out in the darkness.

"What are you doing out here?"

"Right now, I'm helping you, and getting rained on. Let's get you back inside. You don't look so good."

"I'm tired."

"I bet," the gunslinger said as Gilbert collapsed back into the lean-to.

CHAPTER 26 | DOUBT

"Whoa—whoa! What?" Gilbert awoke from a startling dream. It was slightly lighter, almost dawn.

"You all right?" the gunslinger said as Gilbert jerked awake.

Gilbert snapped up, looking over at the guy, surprised he was real. "I— I'm— Are you a park ranger or something?" Gilbert asked, breathing heavily in a fevered wheeze.

"Listen to you. You sound crazy. What the hell are you doing here? Look at those tarpaper clothes you have."

"I'm—"

"What kind of hand are you playing?"

Gilbert scratched behind his ear and furrowed his eyebrows, confused. "Why would you say that? Is that what this is about?"

"What is *what* about?" the gunslinger asked, cocking his head.

"Are you with Jimmy Dove?"

"Jimmy Dove?"

"You look like some Old West gunslinger."

"Gunslinger? Do I?"

"Do you have a gun under that coat?"

"Well, that's a personal question, isn't it?"

"Do you?"

"Why do you care?"

"Do you?"

"Do you want me to have a gun?"

"I don't know."

"Do you wish *you* had a gun?"

"*Me?*"

"Yeah, you. You see anybody else out here?"

"Yes."

"Yes, what?"

"Yes, I wish I had a gun."

"Why?"

"To kill Trent—to start."

"There it is."

"No, no," Gilbert said, shaking his head. He was confused. His head felt like a cement mixer. "That's not what I'm saying. I'm sorry. I just— This was crazy. He stabbed me. We need to call someone. I don't know what the hell to do." He looked down at the stab wound and the bite on his calf and his burned belly. The bandages and his white underwear were now a rose shade of pink, like the breast cancer awareness bandanas Gilbert and

Jeannie had from an event at her hospital. He stared at his bandages and nearly passed out. "Are you— are you one of them?" he said as he wobbled in his seat.

"You look tired," the man said. "I'm just here to help you if you want it. I don't want any trouble."

"What's your name?" Gilbert asked, looking up at him.

"Buck," the man said. "Pleas'ta meet you."

"I'm Gilbert. Do you have any blankets?"

"Do you really think you could kill a man?" Buck said, ignoring the question.

"No. I wasn't— You don't understand. There's a lot more to it."

"Oh," Buck said with a chuckle. "I don't have anything but this raggedy old jacket, but I'll share it with you when you need it. Fair enough?"

Gilbert nodded, growing more and more confused.

"Why don't you get some rest till sunrise. I'll keep a watch."

CHAPTER 27 | KIN

GILBERT LOUNGED ACROSS the sofa in his mesh shorts and Bob Seger t-shirt. *High Plains Drifter* was playing on the TV, a Saturday morning summer special: a Clint Eastwood Western marathon, interrupted only once an hour by a block of commercials—all of which were summer themed, about beers on the beaches and boat sales and town festivals, stuff like that. Great way to spend a Saturday. It was almost noon, and it was hot. The windows were open and the air moved through in a pleasant way, even as hot as it was. He had nothing to do all day, and nothing sounded better than a Clint Eastwood marathon and very, very little movement.

The High Plains Drifter was just about to save the townsfolk of Lago from the criminal hooligans when Jeannie rushed out into the living room on her cell phone, frowning, not exactly looking at Gilbert, totally focused on the phone, but still trying to get his attention. "Just slow down, Liz," she said. "Where are you?"

Something had happened. He could see that. He wouldn't be finishing the Clint Eastwood marathon that day. He knew that. If this were a real marathon, he'd just pulled his hamstring.

Gilbert muted the TV and sat up and motioned with his face to Jeannie to ask what was up. She just shook her head in an apologetic way and held up her finger for more time. Gilbert sat back into the couch and watched Jeannie.

Ten minutes later she hung up the phone and immediately gave Gilbert a look to say, *I'm sorry.*

"I'm sorry, Gubby," she said out loud after saying it silently for a long moment.

"What's up? Is Liz okay?"

"She's fine, I think. Just an argument with Trent."

"Oh yeah?"

"I'm sorry, Gubby, but we have to go pick her up."

"That's fine," he said.

"I know you didn't want to do anything today," she said, with the same apologetic look, glancing over at the TV and the High Plains Drifter on mute. "I'll just go myself."

"No, it's fine. I've seen it a million times. Where's Liz?"

"Granville, I think."

"Granville?"

"Trent left her out there," Jeannie said, snarling. "Asshole."

"In Granville?"

"I don't know. I guess they had a fight. I don't know what happened. But she's standing by a farm on Route Eight right now. Out in this heat."

"Let's go. I'll drive."

It took over an hour to reach Liz. When they did, she was sitting in the shade under an oak tree, fiddling with a stick, her makeup streaked with tears. Gilbert didn't look her in the eyes as they got out and she came over and hugged Jeannie and got in the car. Jeannie got into the back with her, and they were quiet for a moment as Gilbert put his little blue Toyota into drive and pulled back out onto the road.

"How you doing, babe?" Jeannie said, turning to her sister and putting a hand on her knee.

"What a fucking asshole," Liz said, tearing up.

Gilbert didn't say a word for the rest of the trip. He just drove the car and stopped at the store when they told him to stop and drove when they told him to drive, letting the sisters talk it through. It took them three hours to get home from what should have been a one-hour drive. But Gilbert was happy to play chauffeur. He had nothing else to do, and he was always impressed with how Jeannie handled these kinds of situations: totally in control, calm, and thoughtful. Always about what can be done. Not wishing things were some other way, but just what was forward, what was next, what was the best decision in the moment. It was one of the many things he loved about her. She could be as sweet and cuddly as a koala when she was in her hot-chocolate-and-slippers winter-coziness routine, but when she had to act, particularly on behalf of her sister or family—or him—she was a laser-guided shark.

Gilbert listened to Jeannie and Liz hash out the situation and drove, watching the forest and farms pass, and despite it all, a smile rose to his lips, at the hot summer day, at the horses in the fields, at the long winding road and the caring and capable wife that he got to call his own, in action, helping her kin.

CHAPTER 28 | ROBOTS

GILBERT AWOKE FEELING better. Marginally better, but better. His injuries were now thick and terrible aches more than sharp contractions of searing fresh wounds.

Buck sat on the edge of the lean-to, stacking a pile of small stones on top of each other. He had five or six stacks, cairns, he called them. He said they help mark trails and junctions, to show you the way. "Looks like it might finally be letting up," he said as he put the final stone on a pile and looked up at the sky.

Gilbert squinted out at the rain and it seemed to be coming down as hard as ever, but he hoped Buck was right. "We need to eat," he said.

"There've got to be some plants to eat around here," Buck said. "I don't know this area very well, but there've got to be some plants."

"What are you doing out here then?"

"Huh?"

"If you don't know the area?"

"I'm just the same as you are: spending some time in the woods."

Gilbert looked down at his hands. "I'm sorry. I just— My friend stabbed me. I mean— He's not my friend— And he never really was. But— I don't know. I just don't know who to trust."

"Can you trust yourself?"

"What do you mean?"

"It's simple."

"Yes, I mean—"

"Then, can you?"

"Yes."

"Then trust yourself to know who to trust."

"You know, Buck. My fucking head hurts, and my whole body, and I don't know if you're talking in riddles, but I can't try to think right now. I think there are acorns around here. Maybe we should just look for those. I don't have a lot of gas left in the tank."

"There we go," Buck said with a smile. "I'm feeling better already. Acorns. That'll do fine."

"Okay," Gilbert said, trying to focus and stand up, finding everything in his body not working right, like all his inner mechanisms were off by a tooth.

They searched out into the rain and found some acorns and broke them open and ate the insides. They were sour and pithy, but it felt good to be chewing on anything. They gathered the acorns into their shirts and went back to the lean-to and crushed them with the rocks from Buck's cairns and ate what they could. It was no meal, and it wouldn't do much, but it was good to work at something that had an edible reward. It was all the body wanted, and Gilbert felt better and stronger during and after.

"We need to get out of here," Gilbert said. "Out of the woods."

"You got that right," Buck said, nodding his head. "You lost some blood."

"Which way were you planning to go before you ran into me?" Gilbert asked.

"Same as you. Like I said. I think the only way is to take Santanoni Ridge. All the other ways are washed out and blocked. You feeling up to it?"

"No," Gilbert said and cracked the smallest grin as he looked up at Buck.

"No shit, partner," Buck said, chuckling. "Me nei-ther."

Gilbert smiled at Buck and they both looked out at the rain for a long moment. Then Buck brushed the acorn shells off the lean-to floor and out into the mud.

They packed up what they had—nothing—and stepped out into the blowing wind and rain. Buck walked up ahead as they left the lean-to. Gilbert followed behind in his tarpaper skirt, vest, and cone hat. On his feet, he wore the asphalt shingle sandals. He grabbed a good stick to use as a walking stick and trudged through the deluge after Buck.

They hadn't gone far when Gilbert stopped. "I don't know if I can make this walk," he said.

"It's just a walk," Buck said. "You were made for it."

"I don't know."

"I *do* know. It's true. You're just a robot made to walk. That's all there is to it. Plain as pure sugar cane. You were made for it, and you'll be fine. Let's go. It's the truth."

"The truth?" Gilbert said and started moving again, one foot in front of the other.

"Just a marching, boning, gold mining robot for the Ancient Leons," Buck said, chuckling and swinging his arms up in front of Gilbert like he was saying something important. "That's all we are."

Gilbert just raised a confused eyebrow. "Leons?"

"That's what they say," Buck said with a grin. "And they're right. The answer is yes— Or forty-two."

"They?"

"Just autonomous marching robots programmed to climb up and dig gold out of the mountains and to replicate, to create and program new gold-mining robots to replace ourselves when our systems start to fail from overuse."

Gilbert chuckled. "Gold-mining robots?"

"That's right. Made to hike up into and out of the mountains where the gold's at, just like we're doing now."

"And to *replicate*?" Gilbert said.

"Reproduce, brother. With vigor. And replace."

Gilbert grinned. "Where'd you say you're from again?"

"Laugh all you want."

"It's not the craziest thing I've ever heard."

"No, sir. And that's why you'll be fine. You can walk up and down these mountains for days if you want to. It's what you're built to do."

Gilbert appreciated the motivational speech, however it came out, and he smiled at Buck. "A little leaky though," he said, nodding down at the stab would and the bite. "But, let's get moving, huh?"

"Let's get moving."

They started walking again and Buck moved up front again, whistling and singing to himself and to the trees and the rain. He walked with a hitched gait, as if guarding an old injury, but he moved with an ease that Gilbert envied at the moment.

Gilbert hobbled behind. The tarpaper was rubbing on his skin even through the plastic, and the shingle sandals were awkward and painful. But it was better than the alternative. Despite the pain of his wounds and discomfort of everything else, he kept putting one foot in front of the other, thinking about what Buck said. It was slow, but after repeating that for a while, he'd covered a quarter mile, then a half, and eventually, he felt like he might actually be able to make it. What he had were the bare essentials, but it was indeed the essentials: it was all he really needed. He could do this, and Buck seemed to know what he was doing. And two is always better than one.

They walked for a long time, gently climbing as they advanced up the foot of the Santanoni range. Buck was a good distance in front at this point, and Gilbert could hear a faint trace of his whistling making its way back through the whipping wind and rain. It was a reassuring sound—the whistling—and Gilbert just shuffled toward it, like a homing beacon, one step, then another.

He only stopped when he needed to, as rarely as possible, and they moved like that for hours. Slowly, but moving.

Later in the day, as Gilbert paused, turning his back to the wind, he lifted his head to wave to Buck, to tell him he had to stop, when he heard a sharp crack from up above, almost like a canned version of the thunder they'd been hearing, but closer, and sharp.

And then the sky was falling.

That first irrupting crack of sound split and splintered into a thousand sharp pops and a thunderous rush as a hundred-year-old pine tree came crashing down through the forest canopy and onto the forest floor with an explosion of branches and debris. The ground shook like an earthquake and rain and branches and needles and leaves pelted down from the sky above, dropping all around the area, the leaves and water spray floating down last onto what suddenly became a silent and eerily still scene.

It looked to Gilbert like the tree fell right on Buck.

CHAPTER 29 | ARBOR

"BUCK!" GILBERT YELLED and stumbled up to the tree as fast as he could. "Buck!"

But there was no response. He thrashed his way around the tree to the other side, searching frantically for any sign of Buck.

"Buck!" he yelled, but heard no response.

He climbed up into and under and through the splayed branches of the tree. He knew Buck had to be underneath, and he dug and burrowed his way through, ripping pieces off his tarpaper clothes and covering himself in cuts and scratches and pine sap. He could do nothing to move the tree, but he tried. He pushed and pulled and shook and hung and yanked and levered and anything he could. But the tree lay dead and unmoving, and no place that he looked did he find any trace of Buck. No hat, no jacket, no handkerchief or boot.

He searched and yelled and screamed—and cried in the end. He paid no attention to time, but when the gray soup in the sky turned an angry shade of steel, Gilbert knew that Buck was dead, and nightfall was coming soon.

Gilbert looked around himself. The forest was endless. He was pretty sure he knew which direction they had been travelling. But after all the running around, he couldn't be certain. Should he leave Buck out here? What should he do? What if he's just unconscious? Gilbert matted his hair forward with his palm a few times and then his shoulders shook under the torn tarpaper and he cried again.

Without any better place, Gilbert crawled into the sprawling tree and found a small screen of shelter. He curled up and cried, and the rain came down without a hitch, the charcoal sky roiling overhead without a good goddamn for a few more human tears into the flood. He cried in the cold arms of that awful tree, and eventually he fell asleep.

<h1 style="text-align:center">CHAPTER 30 | DAWN</h1>

Dawn did not bring an end to the darkness, only the addition of vision, eyes to see the despair. The gray was just as cold and deadly as the black, and Gilbert thought of dying. Of just dying. There in the arms of an already murderous tree. Would it make the pain go away?

He lay despondent for the first hour of daylight. He could feel the presence of Buck's dead body somewhere under the tree at his back. Death could just come, just like that, and he wouldn't have to walk any further on his torn feet in the endless rain.

But as he lay there, with the tree's criminal arms around him, he, for a second, imagined he could feel Jeannie's warm soft belly pressing against his back, her loving arms and chest wrapping him in her warmth. He opened his eyes and thought of what she was doing right then. It was Saturday morning. A week since he'd been away. She had been sleeping alone. Could she have slept at all? *Oh,*

Jeannie! She was crying right then. He knew it. She was his love. He could feel her soft cheeks against his.

He flinched and jerked out of his melancholy. *Get the fuck up,* he told himself. He scrambled and crawled out of the tree and sprang to his feet, screaming out into the forest in a roar.

"Fuuuuucccckkkk yoooouuuuuu!" he screamed. "Fuck you. Fuck you. Fuck you. I will not fucking die out here, you *asshole!*" He grabbed a broken branch that had come down with the tree and started beating the other branches of the tree with it. He swung and swung and hammered and hammered at that tree until he fell over in exhaustion, his weakened body unable to take the strain, the darkness narrowing in from the reaches of his vision as he collapsed to the ground, looking up at the pounding rain.

After he caught his breath, he got to his feet and took a deep breath and matted his hair forward with his palm and gathered what was left of his hat and found a walking stick and started trudging up the slope. *Up, up, up. Just keep going up,* he told himself. *Up is the way for now. The only way is up.*

Gilbert walked—or shuffled—all day, up, and eventually he found a gradually rising hump that he expected was the beginning grade of what would become the ridge of the range. Then he would just need to follow the ridge. It sounded easy—as words. He stopped and ate acorns whenever he could find them and when he couldn't force another step. He'd sit and let his weakened heart pump weakened blood to weakened muscles for only as long as absolutely necessary. Then he'd start moving again—up.

By nightfall, he had gained the ridge below the shoulder and could see some of his way up. The going was slow. He had to pick every step, and as he went up, the terrain became more and more rocky and steep and tangled with bare roots and stones.

That night, after he found a hollow under a bush to rest in, he heard the sound for the first time.

CHAPTER 31 | KNOT

"HE JUST GETS so mad when I try to ask him anything," Liz said.

They were driving home from picking her up on the side of the road in Granville.

"So, what from here, Liz?" Jeannie asked, seriously.

"He's a weak little asshole, anyway, pretending to be a big macho man."

Jeannie frowned and was about to respond when her phone rang. She pulled it out of her purse and her eyes lightened. "I'm sorry, Liz," she said, pointing to the phone, half-questioningly.

Liz waved her hand with a smile as she rolled her eyes and looked out the window, telling Jeannie to go on.

"Hello, this is Jeannie," she said into the phone. "Hello? Hello?" She pulled the phone away and studied the screen and then put it back to her ear. "Hello?"

"Got any reception?" Gilbert whispered.

Jeannie just shrugged her shoulders at Gilbert. "Hello?" she said into the phone again. Then she perked up. "Hello? Hello? Yes— Yes, I can hear you."

Gilbert cocked his head as if to ask who it was, and Jeannie just put up a finger and smiled at him, giving him a thumbs up.

"Hello, Doctor Zimmer," she said into the phone. "I'm sorry. I'm right on the edge of cell coverage."

Gilbert slowed down and pulled the little blue Toyota to the side of the road so she would keep whatever reception she had. He and Liz watched as Jeannie finished the clipped conversation and hung up the phone.

She turned to Gilbert and then to Liz with her eyes wide and her jaw open in smiling surprise.

"What is it?" Liz said.

"Doctor Zimmer wants to meet with me," she said, then pointed at Gilbert. "He wants you and me to meet him and his wife next Saturday at his house up on Brant Lake."

"No way!" Gilbert said, elated for his wife. "That's amazing, Jeannie. Congratulations."

"Nothing to congratulate yet, but—" She trailed off with a wide smile on her face.

"See," Liz said with a sarcastic smile, happy for Jeannie but rolling her eyes in joking jealousy. "You get the good job. You've got good old reliable Gilbert." Then she turned to Gilbert. "You know, Gilbert. Thank you. Thank you for being such a good guy to my sister."

"Thanks," Gilbert muttered, uncomfortably—but he appreciated it.

"You may not be— you know— I mean, you're a really good guy, Gilbert. Thank you."

"I'm sorry this happened to you," Jeannie said to Liz, hugging her sister around the neck. "I love you."

"Love you, too, Jean," Liz said and squeezed her arm. "Thank you."

They dropped Liz off at her parents' house, and her parents thanked Jeannie and Gilbert for helping, and after some small talk and some shit-talk about Trent, Gilbert and Jeannie were back in his little blue Toyota, heading home, just before sunset.

"Let's drive up to the back side of West Mountain and watch the sunset," Jeannie said as Gilbert pulled out of her parents' neighborhood street and onto the main road.

Gilbert just looked over at her and smiled, nodding once. He knew his wife was worried about her sister.

He turned the little blue Toyota onto Vista Road and through the tunnel of giant oak trees as the road departed from the organized grid of suburbs and into a meandering road up into the hills west of town.

Gilbert pulled off at the same place they'd stopped hundreds of times before. They loved to drive, to take a Saturday and find a country road and drive, turning wherever they wanted, trying to get lost on the idyllic byways of the Adirondack Park. But when they needed a view, close to home, this is where they came. The scene from their perch looked out at the blanketed hills and mountains to the west and down at the Hudson River flowing far below, following down its silky path through the forest, the bright orange and pink colors of the sunset shimmering off its surface like an oil painting draining out of the mountains.

Gilbert reached forward and pressed the shutter button on his little dashcam. It took wide angle shots that usually turned out nice on nights like this when the sky was big and bright with a sunset. He adjusted the mount and took another.

"Have you been liking that?" Jeannie asked.

"I love it," he said. "I got an awesome shot of a deer running out in front of me the other day."

"Oh, goodness."

"I didn't hit it."

"Well, that's good at least."

"I was able to zoom in on the deer's face in action later, right in mid-stride, at the moment he saw me barreling down the road at him and shat his pants—tongue out. It was a riot."

Jeannie giggled. "Sounds like it."

"It was. He was like—" Gilbert tried to imitate the shocked look of the deer screaming in the picture. "I sent it to my cousin. He got a kick out of it. Said he's going to make a meme out of it."

"What did it look like again?" Jeannie asked, chuckling at Gilbert's impression.

Gilbert made the face again, and they laughed.

"I'm glad you like it, babe," she said, wiping tears from her eyes.

Gilbert smiled at her, lovingly.

"I love you, Gubby," she said, blinking her eyes. "Thank you for the life we have together."

"Right back at you," he said. "I don't know why you keep me around, but I'm sure glad you do."

She smiled at him and they looked out the windshield and over the forest at the reddening sky as the last pinpoint of the sun's surface dropped behind the mountains in the distance.

CHAPTER 32 | PLEAD

WHEN GILBERT FIRST heard the sound, late that night, he could tell it wasn't far from him. It was far enough that he couldn't distinguish what it was, but it wasn't far. It kept him up and uneasy throughout the night, faint but incessant. Maybe a squirrel? A coyote? A ghost?

A bear?

The night dragged on. He knew he should be walking, but it was so dark. He would have to get over it. He knew that. But he also wanted to sleep. He wanted to be comfortable, sleeping somewhere—not there. He was drained, and in pain. The sound in the near distance played tricks on his mind. It was coming from the direction he was traveling. And whatever it was, he didn't want to find it at night. It didn't sound friendly—for some reason. He didn't know why, but it didn't. So, he pressed his eyes closed and tried to listen to the rain, and the rain granted him its din. But despite the volume and the immersion in the rain, that faint sound wormed its way through. It would stop for periods of time, and Gilbert would rest, but then it would cut through again.

That morning, in the pre-dawn light, the rain had almost stopped and Gilbert rose, exhausted. With nothing else to do, he continued his trek, shuffling closer to the sound. After a short distance, the sound stopped and all was silent but for the drips of water falling off the leaves. He lost the direction and started to doubt if he was even hearing anything, or if the white noise of the forest had formed in the thickening coagulate of his mind into an incessant clacking and howl off in the distance that wasn't really there. For a couple of minutes, he stood in the silence, trying to focus out into the woods, waiting, uncertain.

Then he heard it again. He just caught it in the wind. Maybe a tree creaking? But he shuffled in the direction he thought he heard it and then heard it again. For the next ten minutes, he moved closer, the same direction he had already been traveling, the sound getting louder and louder as he went, but never getting loud.

It was coming from below a rock ledge.

Gilbert took a deep breath and steadied himself and inched closer to the edge, and closer, and closer, until he could peek over the rim.

"Gilbert—"

Gilbert stumbled at the sight and held himself up with his walking stick.

"Gilbert—" the voice said faintly again.

Gilbert just stared, frozen.

"Gilbert. Help me."

Gilbert stepped back from the ledge and over to a small rock sticking up above the lichen and scrub covering the forest floor. He sat on the rock and looked down at his deteriorating makeshift sandals. He palmed his hair forward and sat in silence.

"Gilbert," the voice croaked from below the ledge, out of sight. "Gilbert, are you there?"

Gilbert picked at the ground in front of him as he huddled on his rock. He poked at it with his finger and tore at the tiny vegetation. The deathly gray clouds were right above him now, right on his head, pressing down on him, the cold mist of the cloud's undulating belly striking out through the drizzle, mixing with the atmosphere like a sickness, adding sting to the bite of the saturated gusts of wind. He dug at the ground with a four-inch piece of broken stick he uncovered under the moss.

"Gilbert—" came the croak. "Gilbert, are you there?"

Gilbert pressed his hair forward and stood up, not looking back toward the ledge. He repositioned his cone hat back on his head and stepped away from the rock he had been sitting on, turning his back to the ledge and the sound, and walking out into the forest.

CHAPTER 33 | ROCK

TWENTY MINUTES LATER, Gilbert picked his way through the giant boulders. There was no flat ground to step on. He had to leave his walking stick behind, and the weight on his wounded calf shot shivers of pain up and down his leg. He picked his way through the boulders and along a narrow outcropping, and eventually found what he was looking for.

He stopped when he saw it, and his mouth twisted into a frown. "What happened?" he said, monotone.

"Gilbert! Oh, God, Gilbert!"

"What happened?"

"I fell, Gilbert. Oh, Gilbert. Help me. I don't want to die."

"You tried to kill me."

"No, Gilly, no. No, I just— I was out of my mind. Oh, God, Gilbert."

"Don't call me Gilly."

"No, no, of course not. I'm sorry. No more calling you Gilly. Okay? No more calling you Gilly. Oh, man, Gilbert, I'm sorry."

"You tried to kill me, Trent. You may *have* killed me. I don't know if I'll make it off of this fucking mountain. I don't even know where I am."

"Yeah, see, Gilbert, you need me. I know the way."

"No, Trent."

"Yes, yes you do. Please? You need to help me. You need my help."

"No. I need your map. That's all I need."

"What?"

"Your map, Trent. Give it to me."

"No, Gilbert, no. You have to help me."

"Give me the map, Trent. And the knife. Throw them over."

"Come and get them, you little son of a bitch!" he snarled and writhed around on the ground, grabbing the knife out of his t-shirt breast pocket. "I can take you with a broken leg and a whole lot more, you little *bitch*!"

Gilbert just stared at him without any emotion showing on his face. He looked at the white bone protruding out of the skin over the area that used to be Trent's shin. He silently walked over, and with a small struggle, picked up an angled rock about the size of a soccer ball from a pile below the ledge. With an expressionless glance down at Trent, he shuffled over to a small boulder right above Trent's head and climbed up onto it.

"What— what the hell are you doing?" Trent stuttered, fear washing over his face and wiping any trace of bravado from his voice. His eyes followed Gilbert with growing anxiety. "Gilbert."

Gilbert didn't say a word. He grunted as he stepped up onto the two-foot-tall boulder. On top, he positioned himself and struggled with the heavy rock until it was held out in front of him, directly over Trent's head.

"What the—?" Trent squealed, squirming around below it. "What are you—? Stop it! I'll give you the damn knife and map."

"Throw them over there," Gilbert said, tracking Trent's head with the rock, which was now shaking in his outstretched arms. "I can't hold it much longer."

"What the fuck, Gilbert?" Trent shouted, throwing the knife and scrambling to pull the map out of his pants pocket—Gilbert's pants pocket. He threw the map over with the knife at exactly the same time the rock let loose of Gilbert's grip.

The rock came crashing down just beside Trent's head. With a slight, deliberate shift just before he let go of the rock, Gilbert had saved Trent from having his brain smashed all over the wet granite of that nameless ledge. Now he walked over to the map and knife and picked them up and walked away, rounding the corner out of sight and picking his way along the rocks below the ledge until he got back to where he left his walking stick.

"Gilbert!" Trent called as he walked away. "Gilbert! Gilbert! Don't leave me, Gilbert!"

CHAPTER 34 | BEARING

BACK WHERE HE left his walking stick, Gilbert sat down beside a tree and unfolded the map. It was almost impossible to know which direction he was facing due to the constant, unending cloud cover. He knew the sun rose in the east and set in the west, but with that godawful muck, the sky was just an avalanche that never stopped but only changed its shades of gray depending on the time of day. Still, using the terrain around him and the map, he was able to make a guess at which direction to move. He hadn't found any acorns in a while, and those from before did nothing to stave his hunger. He knew there was probably something else he could eat out there, but he didn't know what. He closed his eyes and pictured his overstuffed leather recliner at home. It had duct tape on the leg from overuse, but the beautiful swale that he sunk into every time he sat down was from overuse as well, so the chair stayed. Jeannie hated it. But she smiled and laughed about it. Even if that chair was the most uncomfortable thing in the world, he still would have kept it just for that, to see her smile and laugh about it. He'd grab her by her flowered blouse and pull her over to him. Pulling on the back pocket of her jeans until her rump landed into his lap, the chair creaking with the two full-sized humans in love.

"You love it," he'd say.

"I love you, Gilbert," she'd say with the playful grin that made him melt. "But I do *not* love this chair."

"Do you still love me in the chair?"

"For all time."

"You're crazy."

"A little."

He'd hold her into him then. There wasn't another thing in the world. He couldn't even imagine being in the same room for a long silent moment with any other person on earth, but from the first moment he ever touched Jeannie, he felt like he could hold her forever and never let go, never say a word, and never need to. Her soft skin radiated a calmness and warmth that sent him to another place. It was like when they flip the sharks on their backs during Shark Week, was how he thought of it. Tonic immobility they called that. He joked with her that her loving touch was like flipping the shark. And of course, he was the shark. Gubby the shark—the poker shark, he liked to think.

"My Gubby shark," she'd say, tickling his sides and sending him into fits that would launch her off him and both of them out of the deep hollow of that old leather reclining chair, laughing and giggling and wiping humor's tears.

He could practically smell the cookies she was baking. Maybe it was Christmas time. Maybe the middle of January, on the coldest day of the year, dark in the afternoon, and the fire going and a chill reaching in from the windows so they'd have to stay to the middle, hugging and touching and embracing at every chance, the hot cookies from the oven burning their lips, spilling hot chocolate down their chins.

Gilbert came to in the driving rain. The sky had darkened again, though it was only around noon, he guessed, and he could see his faint breath in front of him, drifting away from its dying host to be battered and broken up by the cold, biting downpour. His bare legs were out in front of him, sticking out of his tarpaper skirt and turning a ghastly shade of blue everywhere but the area around the loose flap of flesh being held to the rest of his leg by the makeshift cotton bandage. He could feel the stab wound in his side, below his tarpaper vest, throbbing with every pitiful beat of his heart. He imagined it looked a lot like the area around the wound on his leg: red and blue with black death shriveling in from the edges of the wound, white puss and pink blood oozing out from unseen locations under the bandage.

He leaned his head back against the tree and squeezed his eyes closed and began to cry.

"Well, that sure ain't the most heartening sight you've ever seen in your life."

"What?" Gilbert snapped his head toward the voice.

"Probably not exactly the time you'd want me to walk up, huh, partner?"

"Buck!" Gilbert shouted, springing to his feet— as much as he could *spring*. "You're alive!"

"Don't know if I feel like it," he said, wiping his brow. His eyes looked tired.

"I thought you were dead."

"Me, too," he said.

"Where the hell were you?"

"Well, cowboy, don't look now, but I'm afraid you misunderstood the nature of our relationship."

"Why? I searched for you."

"I didn't ask you to do that."

Gilbert palmed his hair forward on his head and looked down at his toes, confused.

"Did you know that of the billions of organisms on planet earth, humans and housecats are the only two that will kill just for the fun of it?" Buck said. "Isn't that odd?"

Gilbert just looked at him.

"I'd say the housecats should get a pass because they're probably just mimicking our behavior," Buck said.

"Do you have any food?"

"Do you also know that while people are perfectly

fine with watching a human get killed or tortured in a movie or stage play, they aren't okay with seeing animals harmed at all in these entertainments? Not even a little bit. Even if it's just a fictional movie and no animals get actually hurt in the production. They'll watch war movies and movies dedicated to the torture of humans, even real documentaries showing real humans being killed, seeing every detail, but even hint at one kitty cat getting its cute little head sawed off with a Swiss army knife and you'll lose your audience for good."

"Good Lord, man."

"See." He laughed and looked out into the woods. "I'm sorry. I say stupid things. I've been a little starved for conversation. And you look like you need to get your mind off of things."

"And put that kind of picture in my head instead?"

Buck stopped and looked down at Gilbert, turning serious. "Why you sitting here crying, partner?" he said with genuine concern.

"I don't know what the hell to do."

"You don't know which way to go?"

"I think I know which way to go."

"Then what don't you know?"

"I don't know."

"Well," Buck said with a chuckle, looking up at the trees. "I guess that's the truth, ain't it?"

Gilbert just looked up at him.

"I'm-a just keep on slogging up this trail then, partner. Good luck figuring it out."

"Wait, what? You can't leave."

"Sure can. I've got a life worth saving, young brother. I've got to keep moving. I'll scout up ahead for you. If I see anything, I'll leave a sign."

"No. No, you can't."

"You'd slow me down anyway."

"You can't."

"Then get up off your ass," Buck said and turned and lumbered through the brush and out into the multiplying mist.

"Buck," Gilbert said, almost to himself. "My friend needs help, too." But Buck was gone into the fog and Gilbert didn't get up and chase after him.

For a few long moments Gilbert sat and looked at his hands. They were brown and dirty and covered with blood. His skin was deformed from the constant wet. He wiped his hands on his tarpaper skirt and then brushed his hair forward with his palm.

CHAPTER 35 | LEDGES

"ARE YOU GONNA drop another goddamn rock on me?"

Gilbert stood there in his tarpaper suit with his shrinking belly stuck out in front of him. He was looking at the ground between him and Trent, frowning. "I'm going to help you, Trent," he said, palming his hair forward. "Even after what you did."

"Yes. Yes, I appreciate it, Gilbert. I know I don't deserve it. Thank you. Thank you. You're no murderer, Gilbert. And that's what it would be."

Gilbert screwed up his eyes and stared Trent straight in the face.

"I'm just saying," Trent said, holding up his hands.

"I'm going to have to set that leg," Gilbert said, nodding down at the injury.

Trent's attention shifted to his leg, and his hopeful smile turned to horror. "Have you ever done something like that?"

"No."

*

FORTY-FIVE MINUTES LATER, Trent was passed out from the pain, but his leg was back to a relatively straight orientation and was wrapped in a tarpaper splint with two sticks on each side for support. As Trent lay unconscious, Gilbert fashioned him a crutch from the length and notch in a downed branch.

When Trent rustled, Gilbert moved over to his side.

Trent jerked awake and immediately looked down at his leg, screaming.

"It's okay. It's okay," Gilbert said, placing a calming hand on his shoulder.

"Oh, God. How did it go?"

"It looks good under the splint," Gilbert lied. "Can you sit up?"

"I think so," he said and raised himself to his elbows with an uncomfortable grunt, but not a howl.

Gilbert held up the crutch, as a question.

"I think I can," Trent said.

"First we have to get you up over that ledge you came down."

Trent looked up at the ledge, terrified. "Can I make it out the way you came in?" he said, motioning to the narrow ledge behind Gilbert.

"I don't think so. I can barely get through with two decent legs. But I think we can get you up over there," he said, pointing over to a five-foot boulder below the ten-foot ledge. "Your arms still work, right?"

"My arms are fine."

"I'll prop you up against that boulder, and then if I get up there and pull, we can probably get you up to the top of that, and then do the same up to the top of the ledge."

Trent nodded and held his hands up for Gilbert to help him up.

Gilbert stepped over and with a slight hesitation bent down and slid his arm under Trent's and grabbed him to pick him up.

Though utilitarian, it was a hug, and they were close, and he could smell Trent, and their cheeks touched, and he could feel Trent's rough stubble, and he dropped him.

Trent howled, gulping between breaths.

"I'm sorry. I'm sorry. Here, I've got you." Gilbert reached down and hugged him again and this time they got Trent standing on his one good leg.

Trent balanced and breathed. "Makes my leg throb being vertical."

"Better than being dead," Gilbert said with a grunt as he held Trent up. "Here, take the crutch."

Trent took the crutch and held himself steady.

With a great deal of effort, Gilbert clambered up

onto the rock behind Trent. He was not swift under the best of circumstances, and with his injuries and dwindling energy reserves, he struggled. But eventually, he made it up to the top.

"You ready?" he asked when he got set.

"I guess," Trent said. "Will you be able to do this?"

Gilbert stood up and looked down with a mix of impatience and uncertainty, hurt, like when he'd be picked last for everything by people like Trent. That one question made him doubt himself, made him unsure if he could do it. A few minutes earlier, he'd steeled himself to the task of setting the leg and getting Trent up the ledge, to try to save his life—maybe. At that time, he was sure he could. But with one hint of doubt as he stood up on that ledge, he was again unsure.

"I don't fucking know, Trent," he said, flopping his hands to his side and frowning. "What do you think we should do?"

Trent looked around, and the options were slim. He tilted his head back and forth and sighed deeply, obviously studying the lack of options. "I think your plan is the best option we have, Gilbert. We can do it."

"Do you want to come up forward or backward?"

"I think forward will hurt like hell on my leg, but it gives us the best chance because I can use my arms better."

"I'll try to reach down and grab you by the back of your pants," Gilbert said.

As soon as he said the word *pants*, they both sub-consciously stopped and stared at whatever they had been looking at, eyeing each other out of the corners of their eyes, neither looking at Gilbert's pants on Trent's legs.

After a tense moment, Trent looked up at Gilbert with his head held down and his eyes not reaching all the way up to Gilbert's. "I'm sorry, Gilbert."

"I know, Trent. Let's just do this."

"You can have the pants and boots back up there."

"Come on. Let's go. Grab onto this spot," Gilbert said and pointed to a handhold.

Trent grabbed the handhold and started to pull himself up as Gilbert grabbed him first under the shoulders and then by the back of the pants until they had him up on the rock. Trent screamed in pain as gravity bent his broken leg the wrong way under him, but he kept pulling and made it up, and then caught his breath.

"This one should be easier," Gilbert said about the slightly shorter distance from the top of the boulder to the ledge above them.

Trent looked at it and at his leg and frowned.

CHAPTER 36 | RESTART

THE SECOND LEDGE wasn't a picnic, but it was slightly shorter and there were better handholds, so they had Trent up, screaming in pain, after only a short struggle.

They both lay on the ground after the ordeal, catching their breath, looking up at the sky through the rain.

"Thank you, Gilbert," Trent said when the pain subsided. "You saved my life."

"Not yet," Gilbert said.

"We can do this."

"Let's look at the map. It's going to be a tough climb with that leg."

"We can do it."

Gilbert pulled out the map and moved over close to Trent so he could see, too.

"Where do you think we are?" he asked.

"We're on Couchsachraga Peak," Trent sounded

out the name with a nod of his head, pointing to the peak on the map. "We have to follow the ridge to Panther Peak and then over Santanoni Peak."

"Then it's downhill from there?" Gilbert asked, nodding at the map.

"That's right. Smooth sailing."

Gilbert didn't have the energy to laugh or grin. It was sometime in the afternoon and though the rain had let up some, the sky was darkening by the minute and his stomach was on fire with hunger. He dared not mention his hunger in front of Trent, but he knew he had to find them something to eat. It had been over seven days since they last ate anything substantial, sitting by a beautiful river in a warm lean-to, eating fresh-caught brook trout cooked over an open fire. He could taste the butter, the char from the fire. He didn't even like fish, but he couldn't shake the thought of those fresh fish. His last real meal. A week ago.

"We need shelter for the night, Trent," Gilbert said.

"We should just keep moving," Trent said.

"In the night?"

"We can't go anything but slow anyway, so we'll be able to see fine. There should be a little moon lighting up the backside of these clouds, maybe even coming through in spots."

"We need shelter."

"I've been lying on my damn back for two days.

We need to move. And it's the best way to keep warm, to keep alive."

Gilbert frowned and looked at his toes, his forehead creasing. He palmed his hair forward and didn't say anything.

"Let's just try," Trent said, turning his palms up to the sky. "If we come across a great shelter, we'll take it, but if not, let's just keep moving. I'm dying. And I'm fucking starving. I haven't eaten anything since—"

Gilbert stopped moving and looked down at his side, where his wound was festering under the tarpaper. "You stabbed me for that," he said to Trent without looking at him.

Trent shook his head. "I know, Gilbert. I know. I'm sorry. We need to let that go."

"You may have fucking killed me, Trent. I don't know if it's infected under there. I may be dying. It hurts like hell."

Trent just looked at him, his eyebrows raised with worry. "You want me to take a look at it? I'm no doctor, but maybe I should take a look."

"I don't think so. Let's just get moving."

Trent watched Gilbert with his eyes still hanging in concern. "Why don't you take the pants and boots," he said.

Gilbert looked over at his boots on Trent's feet. Trent started untying the one off of his good foot, and Gilbert held up his hand.

"Don't," he said. "You keep the good one. You'll need it. But if you think we can get that boot off your bad leg, then I'll take it."

Trent looked down at his leg and clenched his jaw, nodding once to Gilbert.

Gilbert knelt down beside Trent and tried to untie the boot as gently as possible with icy, shaking hands.

"Walk a mile in his shoes," Trent said quietly.

Gilbert unlaced the boot entirely to pull it off without moving Trent's foot, and when the time came, he nodded to Trent and Trent nodded back and Gilbert applied the tiniest of pressure to dispossess the foot from the boot. The boot pulled off easily and Trent clenched, but didn't scream, and they both sat back and exhaled, Gilbert looking at his left boot. He tossed away the makeshift sandal from his foot and pulled the boot on and tested it on the ground, smiling as he did.

"According to Mister Handey," Gilbert said. "When you're in conflict with someone, you should walk a mile in his shoes—that way, you're a mile away from him, and you've got his shoes." Gilbert loved telling Jeannie that joke. She'd always laugh. But in this moment, after someone had done to him the very thing the joke was about, the joke hung in the air, and both he and Trent chuckled awkwardly.

CHAPTER 37 | AMBIENCE

LATER, AS THEY shuffled along, the rain returned and Gilbert's mind focused on the sound of the drops on his tarpaper hat. If the rain wasn't killing him and driving him crazy at the same time, the sound of the drops on his hat might have been peaceful. A cool summer's evening, rain clouds rolling in, the leading drops of the storm pinging off the tin awning overhead—at a pizza shop. Gilbert's eyes glazed over as he tried to warm himself with these thoughts. He thought of a similar summer's evening at Doctor Zimmer's house on Brant Lake, where he and Jeannie went a week after the incident with Liz in Granville.

Doctor Zimmer's cottage, as the rich folks called them, was a five thousand square-foot mountain of logs and glass made into a lakeside mansion. He had invited Jeannie and Gilbert up there to try to convince Jeannie to take his job offer. It was a great affirmation of her hard work and Jeannie had wanted to work for him for a long time. He was the best pediatric surgeon in upstate New York, who was now opening a whole new pediatric hospital, and she was a tangle of nerves. Gilbert tried to distract her with small talk as he drove his little blue Toyota through the tall pines and colorful hardwood trees on the lake road around the north inlet of Brant Lake, leading to the house.

As Gilbert and Jeannie pulled up the drive, the many flowers of summer colored the sunspots and filtered shade along the simple gravel driveway leading to the massive log home. Doctor and Lady Zimmer were on the lake side of their home, and Lady Zimmer stepped around the corner of the building to wave Jeannie and Gilbert over to that side of the driveway.

Gilbert parked and they got out and picked their way around the house on a beautiful natural bluestone path that opened into an enormous patio of the same that fell off into a perfectly manicured green lawn running slightly downhill to the tranquil waters of Brant Lake's northern shore.

"Sorry to make you run around the house, y'all," Lady Zimmer said with a bright smile and an embracing nook to her arm as Jeannie and Gilbert drew close. She kissed Jeannie on the cheek and held out her hand to Gilbert, her hand like a tiny bird's wing—held with the fingers down and the wrist up. Gilbert took hold of it with his thumb and forefinger and gave it an awkward shake and nodded his head and looked down at his wiggling toes in their green wool socks sticking out the end of his fraying sandals. *This may be the worst kind of torture*, he thought.

Doctor Zimmer was striding up from the boathouse down by the lake, waving his giant hand over his head.

"Gilbert," he yelled. "Gilbert. I've been trying to get you out here."

Jeannie smiled at Gilbert and squeezed his arm in encouragement. He loved her because she knew how hard this stuff was for him, but she loved him anyway and always made sure he knew she was there to pull him through it.

"Looks like Marty wants to hire you both," Lady Zimmer joked, placing a fond hand on the back of Jeannie's hand and patting it like a mother. "He can't keep his mind off those cards, Gilbert. I think you're his hero."

Gilbert tried his best to smile as he chuckled awkwardly and palmed his hair forward. He alone could sense the slight loving laughter that rose to Jeannie's eyes as she looked at him. He knew she would poke him in the ribs from the passenger seat as he was driving home later that night. She'd grin, and her soft, round grin would grow in her rosy cheeks until it turned into a rolling sweet laughter.

"I can't believe I survived," Gilbert said later that night as he laughed with his wife. "How are you supposed to shake a hand like that? Should I have kissed it?"

Jeannie looked at him with tears of laughter in her eyes. "Yeah, definitely," she said, and burst out laughing.

"That's what I'm going to do from now on," Gilbert said, wiping the tears from his eyes so he could see the road. "I'll just grab hold and lay a big smacker right there on her hand. Good evening to you, Madame!"

"Oh, God, Gilbert. Please do that."

"For three foot rubs," Gilbert bargained, pinching Jeannie in her side as he tried to keep their little blue Toyota on the dark and wet Adirondack road.

Back on the lawn of the mansion, before Gilbert was free to laugh about it in the car on the way home, Doctor Zimmer had corralled him with his large arm.

"Gilbert," he said in his booming voice. "I need some hints." Doctor Zimmer's thinning hair and loosely-buttoned white linen shirt were flapping in the breeze and he was wiping his hands on a mechanics rag with the grease of his most recent project ground into its fibers. "I'm getting killed in my poker game up here. It's brutal. And it's at my house so I have to sit there the rest of the night and sulk."

"No," Lady Zimmer said with a grin. "He comes up and bothers me. But," she paused and held up her finger with a stern authority, "I will not allow us to start the conversation on your boys' games. No offense, Gilbert."

Gilbert just nodded his head and palmed his hair forward, looking at his toes.

"Of course," Doctor Zimmer said, bowing to his wife.

"We'll go inside in a little bit and talk business," Lady Zimmer said. "But they say there's rain coming, so let's enjoy the sunshine while we've got it." She held her arms out to her side to guide the bunch down toward the dock and the boat house.

An hour or so later, when the first plops of rain hit the glassy smooth waters of Brant Lake, Lady Zimmer corralled them again, and they all scrambled to grab towels and phones and sunglasses as they made their way to the house, hurrying in the jovial non-hurried way one hurries from a warm summer shower while at the lake. Gilbert just followed Jeannie and did what he was told.

On the way up the lawn, he slowed and turned to look back at the rain making its way across the lake. It was beautiful. The air was still warm and rich with living foliage and the scent of summer flowers amid a smattering of fallen leaves. The rain came up the lake like a wall. They were only feeling the vanguard blowing out in front of the real rain, a downpour that would hit within minutes.

"Beautiful," Gilbert said to Doctor Zimmer, looking past him at the rain coming across the lake.

Doctor Zimmer was taking up the rear, fiddling with the wires of a portable battery jump-kit as he walked up the lawn behind the other three. He turned to see what Gilbert was looking at as he kept moving up the lawn.

Gilbert stood there looking back at the summer shower now splattering off the front pilings of the dock. The rings in the lake from each drop grew bigger and bigger until in just a few seconds the water was a turbulent mix of impact craters folding into and over one another.

"It sure is," Doctor Zimmer said with a grin as he reached Gilbert, looking back with him at the lake and sighing contentedly. "Come on inside," he said after a second. "I got to show you something."

Inside, Lady Zimmer took all their rain-dampened towels and disappeared while Doctor Zimmer waved Gilbert over to a panel in the wall like a child excited to show a toy. The interior of the house was an architecturally eclectic grand timber design adorned with wood, steel, stone, and tile all mixed and matched masterfully and muted by plush decorations, furniture, and interior plants. The air was warm, dry, and comfortable.

"Check this out," Doctor Zimmer said and pressed a button on a small touchscreen built into the wall. As he did, it sounded as if someone had opened all the windows at once. Before he pressed the button, the house was quiet and the only signs of the intensifying rain outside were the streaks running down the thirty-foot-tall, floor-to-ceiling window array, topping out at the peak of the sharp, gabled roof. But, then, when Doctor Zimmer pressed the button, it sounded as if all the walls fell down and they were back out in the rain.

Gilbert found it fascinating. At first, he thought Doctor Zimmer had actually opened the windows with his little device, which would have been interesting in itself, but he was amazed to find out that the windows were still closed and the house was still warm and dry, but somehow, it sounded as if they were right outside in the storm. He thought it might be a rain track on his music player, but then he could hear the plop of a series of drops landing in a whiskey barrel planter on the patio. He watched the eave drop its water and heard every plop as it hit the barrel. He heard the skitter of a squirrel and saw it bounce across a tree limb at the edge of the bluestone patio.

"Wired for sound," Doctor Zimmer said. "There are microphones outside set to pick up the ambient sounds, so on days like today, you can stay nice and toasty, but still hear the sounds of the forest." From the tablet in the wall, he walked over to the oversized hearth fireplace.

"Nice fireplace," Gilbert said. It was a colossal understatement. The mouth of the fireplace gaped five feet tall and wide, and the stones surrounding it ran five feet to each side. There was an enormous ship's timber mantle that ran the whole width of the stone. Above the mantle, the natural stone tapered up to the peak of the ceiling, still eight feet wide when it burst through the roof.

"We don't do fake fires around here," Doctor Zimmer said, nodding down at the empty grate in the fireplace as Gilbert gawked above them at the stone chimney. "Hope you don't mind a little waft of smoke as it gets its draw," Doctor Zimmer said as he bent down and tossed a starter bundle into the fireplace. He tossed a pile of kindling and logs on top of it, then lit the fire starter with a grill lighter, and within a couple of minutes had a roaring fire going. The three sat on the two couches facing the fire and all stared into the flames for a long peaceful moment before anyone spoke, listening to the warm fire crackle while hearing the dropping of the rain and the roll of the thunder happening just outside the well-insulated walls and windows, the wilderness playing through surround sound speakers.

It was only maybe a few minutes that they sat there like that before Lady Zimmer returned from the laundry room and resumed the conversation. But that moment of tranquility, Gilbert and Jeannie sitting close to each other with the chilly toes of barefoot summer afternoons being warmed by the fire and their proximity to each other, felt like a recharge for the soul. He remembered just staring into that fire and listening to that rain and feeling a wave of relaxation—even being among strangers. He sank into the couch and focused deeper on the flames as the pounding rain entered into his head and became a soft internal drumbeat that weighted his eyes and lightened his legs.

But back in the forest, Gilbert listened to the steady plop of rain on his tarpaper hat and looked at the streak of bloody pink water running down his leg from under his tarpaper armor and felt like he weighed a thousand pounds. He listened to the rain and recalled that day at Doctor Zimmer's lake house and the Doctor's ambient outdoor audio set up. He shook the thoughts of the warm couch and Jeannie from his head and held Trent around his waist so Trent could lean on his shoulder and steady himself as they limped up through the clouds along the spine of Panther Peak toward its summit and the summit of Santanoni Peak beyond.

The going was slow.

"You ever been to Josie's in Lake George?" Trent asked later, as they inched along.

"The burger place?"

"Oh, man."

"I thought we weren't going to talk about food."

Trent shook his head. "Fine, Gilbert. You ever been out on the steamboats there, then?"

Gilbert didn't answer for a minute. "I just think that talking about that kind of stuff is bad for us right now."

"Bad for us? Look at us, Gilbert. We're barely alive."

"I just— I don't know."

"What the hell do you want to talk about? Dying up here on this ridge?"

Gilbert didn't say anything. He just looked down at his one shoe and shuffled along, one step at a time.

"I think it's better to talk about nice things at a time like this," Trent said and then paused, looking down at his one shoe. "I don't want to think about dying."

Gilbert felt the festering stab wound in his side and didn't say anything, but just kept shuffling, one foot in front of the next.

The wound was starting to itch, inside—deep inside.

CHAPTER 38 | MADNESS

GILBERT WAS ACTIVELY curling himself under a bush, muttering to himself, deliriously.

They had stopped for rest, and Gilbert was going mad, writhing on the ground, trying to press himself closer and closer to the bush, as if it would heal him.

"What did you say?" Trent said, craning his neck from where he was lying, resting.

Gilbert kept mumbling and grunting as he shook his head and rolled over onto his other side and back, but he didn't acknowledge Trent or look towards him.

They had stopped because they needed rest badly, but they would only rest as long as needed. They had to keep moving.

Gilbert kept babbling.

"Gilbert? Are you saying something?" Trent strained to see him from where he was lying.

Gilbert babbled, growing more and more irritated, but not hearing or understanding Trent or anything else. He squirmed against the bush, trying to use it for cover.

In Gilbert's head, he could feel his own mind turning to soup. His vision swayed whether his eyes were open or closed. He was so fucking hungry, and mad. He could feel his two wounds spreading, like marching death, up his leg and out from his abdomen. But most of all, he was tired, dead tired.

They slept in that clearing for as long as could be expected. Exhausted or not, sleeping in a rainstorm with no shelter and souring wounds is a speedy affair. Exhaustion may knock you out, but the rain and the pain will surely wake you up before long—if you're lucky. And that was the case with Gilbert and Trent.

CHAPTER 39 | PEAK

TRENT WOKE FIRST, howling with pain. The yelp woke Gilbert and he cringed with the sudden rush from the brief warmth of unconsciousness into the pain and downpour of the pitiful remaining fragment of his life. The swelling made any movement ring with pain, and the first thing he did was cry.

Trent was much worse for the night. His skin had turned from a sallow sickly hue to the color of death itself. They needed food.

Gilbert rolled over and looked at Trent. "I'm going to look for food," he said, his face drawn and his mouth remaining open with no energy to close it. "What can we eat out here?"

"I don't really know," Trent said, shrugging absently, looking down at his hands. "I just hike and fish. I don't know about forest edibles and shit. I bring my own food—and catch extra."

They both stared off in opposite directions, thinking about food—desperate, dying.

"I'll see what I can find," Gilbert said, dragging himself to his feet and shuffling out into the forest.

He stumbled around and searched for what felt like hours, looking for anything that even seemed edible. But he couldn't find any oak trees or their acorns or anything else he knew to be food, and he was badly injured and dazed and couldn't focus. He had no idea what he was looking for even if he could focus, so mostly, he just staggered around and hoped. The rain felt like it might have lightened slightly again, but it still fell, and a thick fog slithered under any assemblage of insulation Gilbert attempted in his tarpaper suit.

Sick with dread and frustration—and cold—he walked to try to warm up, and he studied the ground and the bushes and trees for any sign of something to eat. He found nothing. He found himself pitiful.

But with a step over a moss-covered rock, his boot slipped and peeled the moss back, revealing two long shiny earthworms wiggling and writhing from their sudden disinterment.

He looked at the two slimy beings and picked up the piece of moss and peeled it away. There were two more.

"Good enough," he said to himself, making a face. But oddly, his stomach was so enamored with the idea of any food, that the worms looked half-appetizing. "Relativity," he mumbled, "in the world of worms and man."

He held the worms in his hand and sighed as he started back toward Trent. But in a panicked flash, he realized that he didn't know which way he'd come from. He'd been zig-zagging around for a long time, and when he looked around himself, the forest looked the same in every direction.

"Trent," he said, at first as if to himself. Then he yelled louder, "Trent!"

Nothing.

In an instant, terror washed over him. He spun around. "Trent!"

The forest was still, as if everything stopped to further Gilbert's terror, as if all distinguishing signs to his direction had suddenly ducked behind the trees, hiding, waiting for the kill.

Then a sound. Far in the distance. A gunshot? It couldn't have come from where Trent was. He couldn't have walked that far. Buck, maybe? Thunder?

He shuffled in that direction for as long as his lungs and legs could handle, then stopped to listen. The tarpaper made too much noise for him to listen while moving.

Nothing.

He shuffled a little further, less urgent, already knowing it was futile. Which direction had he come from? He looked around himself, trying to see something familiar.

There was a rock, a boulder. Yes, he'd seen that before. Right?

He moved toward the boulder to see it from the other side, from all angles, hoping one angle would make him sure it was a boulder he'd seen an hour earlier.

Then he saw another boulder. It was very similar. Was that the boulder? How many boulders were there? How many had he seen earlier?

A shiver ran through him, tensing every tendon and muscle in a wave that ran out from his center.

He sat by the boulder, now quite certain it was *not* one he remembered seeing earlier. The rain dripped off his hat and over every part of him.

Why did he even care that he'd lost Trent? Trent was only a burden. He'd tried to kill him. Gilbert pushed at the mud at the base of the rock. What the hell was he supposed to do?

Was it because he knew Trent would die? That he would die terribly?

Gilbert scratched at his head under his tarpaper hat and grimaced. Which way? The fog blocked everything.

He tried to remember the old books he read as a kid about the underground railroad, about how to tell direction in the forest. There was no north star, not in his world at that time. All he saw when he looked up were clouds. Moss only grew on the north side of trees. He remembered that. But the moss he could find was growing on all sides of everything.

Then he heard a sound again. Not the same

sound. Was it the same sound as before? No. Not the same sound. It was faint. A yell?

He rose to his feet and moved in that direction.

All he heard as he moved was the scraping and rubbing of the tarpaper. He stopped to listen.

"Gilbert!" he heard, not too far off in the distance. "Gilbert!"

He hobbled toward the voice in as close to a hurry as he could muster. He rounded a knoll and saw Trent lying there against the bushes they had slept beside.

"I thought I got lost," Gilbert said, stopping to catch his breath as he shuffled up.

"I thought you were lost, too," Trent said. "Where were you?"

"Where the fuck do you think I was? I was out in the woods trying to find us food, trying to find *you* food."

"Did you find anything?"

Gilbert held up the earthworms.

"Shit," Trent said. "But, sure, I'll take them. We can probably find more if we need to."

"I figured we try one or two first."

They each took their earthworms in their hands and looked at them. Trent ate his first in one swift move and a grimace. He shivered like he'd taken a shot of Tequila, but then shook his head, and both worms were down.

Gilbert took longer, but eventually he balled the two worms up as best he could and tossed them into his mouth, hoping he could just swallow them down in one shot. But they were too big, and by reflex, he chewed a couple of times before he choked them down. It was unpleasant, to say the least, and he gagged and hacked and almost threw up, but they stayed down.

"Let's get moving," Gilbert said, still fighting to keep the worms down, nauseated by the thought of what was in his stomach—maybe still partially alive—but also warmed by having anything at all in his stomach.

Trent nodded, holding his own worms down.

Gilbert helped Trent make it to his feet and they started up the mountain again. Gilbert used his own walking stick for support, holding Trent around his waist. Trent used the makeshift crutch on one side and Gilbert on the other. Like this, they shuffled until first light, making slow time. After a short break at dawn, they shuffled to what they guessed to be around noon. The worms gave Gilbert a little lift in the morning. To have something in his stomach helped him feel alive again for an hour or so. But by mid-morning, the small amount of food in his stomach was replaced again by pangs of hunger, now more acute.

Around late morning the rain almost stopped and they both looked up at the sky.

"Oh, God, please stop raining," Gilbert said.

The rain seemed to pick back up again as soon as he said that, but a few minutes later it slowed again and then varied on and off for the next few hours until they reached the top of Santanoni Peak.

"They have to be searching for us," Gilbert said as they looked out at the blank clouds still engulfing the summit. They could only see a short distance into the soupy clouds, but they looked down in the direction of the lake, as if some kind of good news just might fly out of the clouds and save them, as if the invisible lake might somehow become visible.

"Maybe," Trent mumbled with a blank stare. "Bad storm."

"We should have left a note at the lean-to, in case anyone finds it," Gilbert said, shaking his head.

Trent made no notice of even hearing Gilbert. He stared out into the clouds, without an expression on his dying face.

Gilbert wondered what was going through Trent's head right then. Trent's look made Gilbert uneasy. He didn't know why, but it did. The mention of the lean-to brought thoughts of the stabbing into Gilbert's head. Did it do the same for Trent?

"Should be downhill from here, right?" Gilbert asked, glancing up at Trent and then back out into the clouds.

But, again, Trent still didn't say anything. He stood there in a dark, brooding haze for a long moment then turned to Gilbert and nodded absently.

CHAPTER 40 | DOWNHILL

THE DOWNHILL SIDE was a little easier, but at times more painful for Trent because of the jolting steps required to move down the slope. They would step and Trent would grimace and they would step and Trent would grimace, and like this, they inched along until the sky started to darken.

Around that time, as they shuffled along, they stepped off a rock just like all the rocks they'd stepped off, on, and around throughout the day, but Gilbert happened to step funny and lose his balance. In doing so, he instinctively reached out to Trent for support, which only succeeded in causing the two of them to both go crashing to the ground.

Trent howled as he hit the ground, and Gilbert screeched with pain as he crashed down and a rock found the wound on his side. They both moaned and writhed around on the ground.

As the pain in his side subsided to a manageable

level, Gilbert looked over at Trent, and he found Trent staring daggers at him.

"I'm sorry," Gilbert said. "I lost my step."

But Trent just scowled with his eyes furrowed in an intense, narrowing focus.

"Maybe we should take a rest here," Gilbert said pulling off his tarpaper hat and palming his hair forward. "Is your leg okay?"

Trent didn't respond but moved to prop himself up. They got him to his feet and silently found a place close by with a log and some bushes to use as shelter. Gilbert helped Trent to a spot on one side of the log and then made his own bed on the other. There would be no warm respite that night. That night's sleep was brought on sharp and cold with shivering exhaustion, and Gilbert faded into the black of a fitful and restless slumber, wholly unaware of the danger lurking behind him in the dark Adirondack forest.

CHAPTER 41 | TEETH

GILBERT AWOKE TO the hot breath of a mountain lion attacking him. There was a split second between the first paw landing on Gilbert's chest and the teeth coming down, in which Gilbert opened his eyes just in time to see the wide jaws of the cat flashing at his neck. The animal came in with its head back like a hammer, or like a snake ready to strike, wide black eyes focusing down his snout at the intended target, ears pressed back. *Just like Snowball when he gets in a mood*, Gilbert thought in the slowed space of that split second.

Gilbert flung his arms up reflexively, and the sudden movement was just enough to save his life. Instead of landing in his neck, the first bite caught his cheek and ear, and opened him up. The next three bites came in a nanosecond, an untraceable blur of jaws and razor-sharp claws as the animal blended his bites to find a kill spot.

Then a shout erupted behind him. "BALLIO, CAT!" Buck yelled and came running out of the forest, faster than you would ever think a cowboy could run. "HOOOO-RAAAHHHH!" he shouted and ran right at the cougar. The cat took no time in deciding and was gone as fast as he showed, disappearing out into the forest.

Buck ran over to Gilbert once the cat was gone. "A mountain lion!" he said, shaking his head in disbelief.

Buck stepped up to Gilbert's side and tried to hide what he was seeing. But Gilbert was a poker player. He made a living reading the thoughts behind someone's nearly imperceptible facial twitches. The slight tensing of the neck, a tightening of the corner of the lips. Buck hid it well, but to Gilbert, it was like looking into a mirror. He knew his wounds were bad.

"He didn't do you any favors with the womens," Buck said. "But I don't think he did you in. I need to go get you help, fast. Try to keep all those cuts clean. And keep moving toward the road. Don't stop moving." He pointed the direction to the road and then took off into the woods and the mist.

"What?" Gilbert said, looking off after Buck. But Buck was gone. "Get help!" he yelled, hoping Buck could hear him.

"What the hell is going on?" Trent shouted, grabbing onto a broken chunk of the downed tree they were sleeping beside to pull himself around the end just in time to see a bloody and shocked Gilbert staring off into the forest, yelling, "Get help!"

"What the hell happened?" Trent asked again,

scrambling to pull himself over to Gilbert as fast as he could.

"A fucking mountain lion," Gilbert said, in shock.

"A mountain lion?" Trent cocked his head, wrinkling his brow.

"I barely woke up in time," Gilbert said, still in a daze, looking out into the forest.

"A mountain lion?" Trent asked again.

"You didn't see him?" Gilbert asked.

Trent just shook his head, studying Gilbert's face with a look of worry.

Gilbert just kept looking out into the forest. "Buck jumped out and scared it off."

"Buck?" Trent asked as he moved to get a better angle at Gilbert's cuts.

"Yeah, he's— I didn't mention him to you earlier because I thought he was gone."

Trent sat up and looked at Gilbert. "You what?"

Gilbert was still in shock. "I thought he was dead first, and then I thought he was gone. He's getting help."

"Dead? He's getting help? What? *Who?*"

Gilbert just turned and looked at Trent, his eyes still wide with shock, his face bloody.

"*Who* is getting help?" Trent asked, shaking Gilbert's arm. "Who?"

Gilbert just looked at him.

"Someone's out here? That can help? What are you talking about? Why didn't you say anything?"

"I thought he was dead."

"Dead?"

"Then— I don't know. He's like a cowboy or something. He was stuck out here, too. I don't fucking know." Gilbert raised his bloodied arm and wiped his face with the back of his forearm, timidly. He looked to the sky and shrugged as he did it, shaking his head and staring off into the distance.

"A cowboy?"

Gilbert looked at the sky for a long time, then came back to earth and looked over at Trent. "Can we focus on my bloody face and the fucking cougar that almost just killed me?"

"Yeah, Gilbert," Trent said, softer, and pulled himself closer to Gilbert to inspect his wounds. He picked up each of Gilbert's arms and then studied the cuts on his face with a few grunts of concern and a few nods of good news.

"Got a couple of good slices that we should wrap, starting with that one on your face, but all things considered, if it was a mountain lion— or bear or something— then you're probably pretty lucky.

"A what?"

"I said it's probably okay."

"It wasn't a fucking bear or anything else, Trent. It was a giant fucking cat."

"Okay, Gilbert. I'm not saying it wasn't."

"Yes, you are."

"Well, come on, Gilbert. What do you want me to say? You know there aren't any mountain lions in the Adirondacks. They haven't been here in over a hundred years."

"There's a least one fucking mountain lion in the Adirondacks, Trent."

Trent just looked at him.

"There *is*," Gilbert said. "And we should be paying attention. He might come back. Didn't you see him? What the hell were you doing?"

Trent held up his hands. "I came as soon as I could. When you started yelling, I woke up. But I thought you were just having a bad dream, and by the time I could pull myself around the tree, I only saw a flash of something run off into the woods—maybe," Trent said. "I don't fucking know. I was facing the other way. I heard some yelling, definitely, yelling from you and maybe an animal, but I can't be sure. I saw something, maybe. But I definitely didn't see any damn cowboy or any mountain cat."

"But you heard him?"

"I heard you."

"And you didn't see the fucking cat either?"

"I thought I saw something, I guess. But I don't know what. It wasn't a cowboy. And I can guarantee you it wasn't a mountain lion."

"Oh, you can guarantee it, huh? What the hell do you think did this to me then?" Gilbert said, pointing to the bloody cuts all over his face and torso.

"I'm sure it was an animal," Trent said, dropping his head, his eyes glancing ever so quickly at the knife folded and clipped to the tarpaper skirt at Gilbert's hip. "I just know there aren't any cougars in the Adirondacks."

"You're a fucking asshole," Gilbert said under his breath, but it was obvious in his voice that at least a hint of doubt was crawling its way through Gilbert's mind.

"Come on, Gilbert. I'm not trying to give you a hard time."

"Just calling me a liar."

"I'm not— I just think maybe it was something else."

"Like what?"

"I don't know, Gilbert. I didn't see it. It obviously cut you up pretty good, so it doesn't matter."

"I'm glad we can agree on that."

"I'm sorry, Gilbert. Let's just get those cuts cleaned up and covered and get moving again."

Gilbert still held his bloodied arms out in front of him—his hands were shaking—and he nodded his head.

They cut pieces of Trent's shirt and the pants as bandages and wrapped the worst of the cuts.

CHAPTER 42 | THOUGHT

"I'VE GOT TO answer this," Jeannie said, looking at her phone and catching her breath from laughing as they drove back from Doctor Zimmer's. "She's called three times."

Gilbert rolled his eyes. "What is it this time?"

Jeannie rolled her eyes and answered the phone. Gilbert watched as her face dropped with worry. "Wait, Liz, slow down. What happened?"

Gilbert looked over, now worried himself.

Jeannie listened mostly, sighing and grunting.

After some further grunting and sighing, she suddenly shook her head and said, "No." She listened, then said no again. But eventually, she sighed and said, "Okay, I'll ask him," and hung up the phone and looked over at Gilbert.

"What's up now?" he asked.

"It's Trent again."

Gilbert frowned. "Do I even want to hear?"

"Oh, Gilbert, I'm sorry."

"What does she want?"

"You're not going to like this."

"Ah, hell, Jeannie. What is it?"

"Don't you *Ah, hell* at me."

"I'm sorry. What did you tell her you'd ask me?"

"You're not going to like it," she said with an apologetic grin.

"You said that already."

CHAPTER 43 | INQUISITION

GILBERT LOOKED LIKE a centuries-dead samurai zombie mummy by the time they were done patching his wounds. He had tiny dirty bloody strips of cotton wrapped and tied around half his body and around his head to keep his cheek and ear in their born orientation. Over this, he had his torn, black, tarpaper top and skirt, like a cheap Halloween version of a samurai's kimono, with the tarpaper cone hat on top and one boot and one shingle sandal on his feet.

"How are you feeling?" Trent asked.

Gilbert just looked at him and then down at himself.

"We should be off the ridge before too long. Then it should get easier."

Gilbert nodded because there wasn't much else to do. He helped Trent to his feet and they continued their shuffle down the mountain, slower even than before. Gilbert could tell Trent was being careful about where he put his hands, trying to avoid the new cuts and gouges, as well as the original stab in his side, and they both were being careful about where they placed their feet so they didn't have a repeat of the crash they'd had the evening before.

"It's fine," Gilbert said as Trent tried to find a good place to put his arm around his shoulders. "The cuts don't hurt too bad. You can put your weight on me."

Trent nodded his thanks and rested his weight on Gilbert's shoulders again.

"How the hell did a mountain lion get out here?" Gilbert said, shaking his head.

"Yeah," Trent said. "I was thinking the same thing."

"It was a fucking mountain lion, Trent."

"Okay, Gilbert. I'm not saying it wasn't. It just— it kind of can't be. They aren't up here. I don't know why we have to argue about it."

Gilbert felt his anger rising, making its way through his weakened and leaking veins and muscles.

"Could it have been a stray dog?"

Gilbert just frowned and looked at their feet as they stepped, and stepped, and stepped.

"Like a big, bad, feral pit bull or something."

"Just shut up, Trent," Gilbert said.

"I'm not trying to give you a hard time. I'm just trying to figure it out. Obviously, something did it to you. You didn't do it to yourself." As he said that last sentence, he glanced over at Gilbert to gauge his reaction.

"Thanks, Trent," Gilbert said.

"Let's just keep an eye out for whatever it was."

"It was a mountain lion, Trent. But whatever you say. Just keep an eye out."

"Maybe, uh—who was it? Buck. Buck. Maybe Buck scared it away."

At this, Gilbert grew angry, the irrational anger that inevitably comes with uncertainty about one's own position. His mind was mush, and there was a growing inverse relationship between how much he thought about something and how sure he was about anything to do with whatever subject that happened to be. He could think clearly about Starburst candy, and cheeseburgers. But anything else came through fuzzy, like old rabbit-ear TVs. The pain and hunger were coming through in HD, but every other line of thought was an old grainy broadcast of *Night of the Living Dead*. He didn't care whether what he said sounded right, or sane. He just wanted Trent to shut the hell up.

"Hey, let's just forget about it," Trent said. "We'll keep an eye out. But let's talk about something else."

Gilbert didn't respond.

"All right. I'm sorry, Gilbert," Trent said, half-sincerely. "I'm not trying to give you a hard time. I'd be dead out here without you to help me. I know that, and I appreciate it."

Gilbert looked up at Trent's face, unsure whether there would be something sour coming next. But there wasn't, and he just nodded, his eyes dropping back to the ground. He didn't know what the hell to think. He was hungry, and he felt like he was dying. That much he knew.

CHAPTER 44 | LEVERAGE

"YOU DON'T REALLY expect me to do this?"

"Come on, Gilbert," Jeannie said. "She doesn't have anyone else she can ask."

"Can't she ask one of *his* friends?"

Jeannie straightened her neck and shook her head. "God, no. None of those guys would do it."

"Exactly," Gilbert pleaded.

"Come on. He respects you."

"No, he doesn't, Jeannie. You know that. And don't patronize me."

"Oh, grumpy Gubby bear," she said with a grin, stepping up to him and tickling him in his ribs, pressing her chest against his arm. "I'm sorry, baby."

Gilbert melted in her arms. She was his world. He sank into the nook of her neck with his arms hanging toward the ground, and she hugged him. They embraced wordlessly for nearly a minute, just standing in the kitchen with eyes closed, drifting on a cloud over the world, just the two of them. Gilbert felt the wave of their embrace travel through his veins from his head to his toes. He fell into a trance and jokingly leaned his weight into his wife, fake-snoring.

Jeannie giggled and held him up for another long moment, the two of them leaning into each other there in their kitchen.

"What the hell am I going to say to him?"

"I don't know, hon. I'm so sorry."

"How does she know where he is?"

Jeannie wrinkled her forehead. "You don't want to know."

Gilbert shook his head. "Come on, Jeannie."

"She tracked his phone."

"Nope. You know what— Nope. Not doing it."

"Come on, Gilbert. She just wants you to talk to him."

"No. She wants me to spy on him. She wants me to track him—probably illegally—to his other girlfriend's house and then confront him."

"No, no. No. She just wants you to talk to him."

"Why? If he's cheating on her, why doesn't she just leave?"

Jeannie shook her head. She couldn't hide her agreement. "She wants kids," she said, spitting it out like it was poison, trailing off as she realized how terrible it sounded.

"Kids? This is crazy. *She's* crazy."

"I know, Gilbert. I know. But you don't know her like I do. She's been through a lot. Okay? And she just doesn't want to have to face this face-to-face."

"Or anything else."

Jeannie fake-sneered at him, then nestled into his side. "Can you just do this, Gubby? It's a favor to me."

With that, it was sealed. Gilbert couldn't say no. Not to Jeannie. He just hung his head and knocked his knuckles on the counter. "You're making me meatballs."

Jeannie's face lit up and she hopped and clapped her hands and kissed Gilbert on the lips. "Thank you, Gilbert."

"Goodness, Jeannie. It's nothing to be excited about."

"Thank you though, Gubby. Liz really appreciates it."

Gilbert rolled his eyes. "Don't thank me. I'll go try to find him. But if I do, I'm going to try to convince him to break it off with Liz and move on out of her life for good. Those two are toxic."

Jeannie just nodded.

"If he's cheating on her, they should not be having kids. Obviously."

Jeannie just nodded.

"Ah, cripes," Gilbert said and threw up his hands.

Jeannie smirked at him, but then turned serious. "Just do what you think is right, Gilbert. I know you will."

Gilbert just shook his head and put his jacket on

with a shrug, grabbing the keys to his little blue Toyota off the hook on the wall.

"Thank you so much for doing this," Jeannie said, leaning into him and kissing his cheek.

Gilbert looked her in the eyes and kissed her on the lips. She tasted like the cookie dough she was mixing and she smelled like the perfume he'd been buying her every Christmas for twelve years. He nuzzled into her neck and enjoyed her scent. Then he stepped back and shook his head and opened the door.

"I love you, Gubby," she said.

"I love you, too," he said and walked out into the night.

CHAPTER 45 | SIGNAL

GILBERT SENSED SOMETHING was wrong before he really knew anything. He was off looking for worms again, or anything else to eat. This time he stayed close to where he'd left Trent, and marked his return trail as he searched. The rain had held off for hours now, and the cloud cover had even gained a yellow hue earlier in the day, at what they estimated to be around noon. It felt to them like a sunny day. Just that slight hint of gold behind the clouds let them know that the sun and a whole world waited beyond the awful gray muck and sky that had been circling them out there in the forest.

The let-up was a long time coming, but as soon as it felt like the sun might break through, might actually start shining, the golden hint disappeared and the clouds turned back to the color of coal. But, even so, the rain held, only dropping a few sprinkles. Their pace had quickened after that, their spirits rejuvenated, marginally; they were still dealing with ghastly injuries and still had a long way to go, and a lake to cross. They could see on the deteriorating map that there was a historic site called Great Camp Santanoni at the southeast shore of Newcomb Lake, where they should come out if they followed the crest of the ridge all the way down. Gilbert remembered that the snowshoers had mentioned it in their journal entry in the first lean-to. Beyond the lake was a road to the main road—and safety.

The problem was getting to the other side of the lake. Newcomb Lake was fed by a series of streams and brooks, all of which would probably be flooded just like the others that had cut them off on the opposite end of their horseshoe trek along Santanoni Ridge. Their working plan was to try to swim across the mouth of one of the brooks, maybe using something as raft for Trent, or to use the island in Newcomb Lake as a waypoint to cross the lake in the middle, the most direct route to the road, cutting off Camp Santanoni.

But first, they had to get to Newcomb Lake. And right now, Gilbert had a bad feeling.

He didn't know if the forest had actually gone quiet or if it was just the lightening of the rain or the tree he was standing under, but he thought he wasn't hearing something that he had been hearing before. He couldn't put his finger on it, but it made his ears perk up. Something had stopped. Was it a bird that stopped chirping? A squirrel that stopped squawking? A woodpecker that stopped pecking? Was it anything? Was his mind going mad? Yes. Of that much he was certain. He was going mad. But what did that leave to trust? Once delusion is established, how can one believe any of it? Hallucinations don't carry red flags above their bikes to let you know they're approaching. They're just there. And to Gilbert Willards, madness was inside, pulling the levers, and he knew it—but it didn't matter. The madness was as much him as he was at that time—maybe more.

He lifted his head again and snapped around.

This time he'd actually heard something. Trent? Was Trent yelling?

Trent was screaming.

Gilbert dropped the rock he was looking under and ran toward the sound.

CHAPTER 46 | PIN

BACK IN JULY, Gilbert drove his little blue Toyota and approached the little red pin showing the destination on his phone's GPS map.

"Ah, hell," he said to himself, suddenly squinting out the windshield. He'd spent the whole ride trying to figure out what the hell he was going to say to Trent if he found him. He still hadn't decided on anything. But he'd been concentrating so much on what to say, that he didn't pay any attention to where the GPS was taking him. He'd only selected the coordinates and hit *Navigate*. Or so he thought. "Fuck," he said when he realized where he was. He must have hit the wrong address or accidentally switched them.

He pulled off the road across from the address and parked. He checked the text message from Jeannie again, and then Google Maps, and they matched. "What the—?" he said, wrinkling his forehead.

He checked the text and the maps four or five

more times, looking around. "What the—?" he kept muttering every time through the circuit, from text, to maps, to front window to back window to the left and to the right, then, "What the—?" And then again from the top. He leaned over in a more and more exaggerated way with every new direction he looked, as if by changing his angle it would somehow change his overall location on the earth, or that some magical sign would pop up in the window and tell him what the fuck was going on. But it didn't, and he just kept going through the progression: text, maps, windows, "What the—?"

After a half-dozen times through, with nothing suddenly showing up differently, he looked down at his phone and pressed Jeannie's name and then the phone icon.

The phone rang twice and Jeannie picked up. "Gilbert?"

"Hi, sweetheart."

"Did you find him?"

"Where did you get that address? Are you sure you got the right one?"

"The address? I think so," she said. "Let me check."

He could hear her shuffling with her phone.

"Any reason why?"

"It may be the right address. And it may confirm something I've been worried about. But I still hope it's the wrong address."

"That doesn't sound good," she said. "What are you talking about? Whose house is it?" Then there was some rustling. "I've got to put you on speaker for a second," she said.

"Yup," Gilbert replied and he could hear her pulling the phone away from her ear and punching buttons. Jeannie always punched at the phone, as if pressing harder on the touchscreen did anything. She'd always giggle and say that it made her *feel* like it was going faster the harder she hit the icons on her screen.

"She only sent me a pin," Jeannie said after a minute. "The coordinates that I sent to you." Jeannie's voice got louder as she pulled the phone closer.

"Shit," Gilbert said.

"What's the matter?"

"Nothing," he said, looking at the large building. "I'll let you know when I get there," he lied and hung up the phone.

He dropped the phone into his lap and shook his head. "Shit," he said once more.

He sat in the car and couldn't decide what to do. Across the street was the unlit entrance to the back of the Sacrament Marina, the same place he'd come for Jimmy Dove's poker game with all the gangsters—where he thought he heard Jimmy Dove mention someone who worked for him named Trent.

He looked at himself in the rearview mirror. "This is the last place you should be snooping around," he said to himself, then turned his eyes out the window toward the back of the marina lot.

Gilbert's little blue Toyota was the only car on the street, under the only street light.

He took a deep breath and sighed as he sat in his car with his belly stuck out in front of him. "Shit," he said to himself, muttering into the darkness.

Play the odds. The range. What makes sense? How much are you willing to risk on what you think you know?

There, looking at the back of the Sacrament Marina, he knew the percentages did not point to innocence—and probably not to an affair either. And the range of possibilities stretched far beyond anything he even wanted to think about. Of course, there was the small chance it could be something entirely innocent. Maybe Trent was doing something for some other kind of work, whatever that might be. Maybe he wasn't the Trent Jimmy mentioned that night. Maybe he was just fishing. Maybe he was cleaning boats. Maybe he was independently wealthy and bought a sailboat and planned to surprise Liz with it as a token of his undying love and they would live happily ever after.

Gilbert didn't think any of those were the case. They were in the range, so he had to consider them, but he didn't get an innocent feeling in his belly, and he'd learned over many nights at the poker table which feelings in his belly to listen to. He knew not to listen at all times.

He knew the belly to be a trickster and a charlatan. But the belly also had its own instinct that you damn well better heed—sometimes. Gilbert had become adept at translating the whispers of his belly, and right now, the belly was yelling that this was perk-your-fucking-ears-up time.

CHAPTER 47 | ATTENTION

As G ILBERT CAME running out to the ledge above where he left Trent, he heard screaming. As he moved into sight of Trent, he saw the mountain lion. It had to be the same one from the night before. The mountain lion had Trent by his bad leg, and was trying to drag him away. Trent was screaming and thrashing at the cat, but each yank from the cat's jaws on his fractured leg set him into convulsions and howls of pain.

Gilbert yelled at the cat and picked up a rock and threw it at it from up on the ledge, missing by a mile. He scrambled down the trail that led down from the ledge, fumbling to unfold the knife as he came out on the same level with Trent and the cat, coming out behind the cat. Down on their level, Gilbert ran at the cat, screaming and waving the knife.

The outburst startled the animal, and it let go of Trent's foot and leapt behind him, spinning to face Gilbert, Trent between them. Gilbert waved his arms and tried to scare it away as Trent dragged himself out of its reach.

The cat hissed at Gilbert, ears back, flat, a tightened rubber band, ready to snap.

Gilbert had run out in a rush to help Trent, but now the cat was turned on him, and he realized that to the animal, he may look like an easier meal than even Trent.

The cat stayed low and circled around to the left of Gilbert.

"No, no," Gilbert said to the cat, holding out the knife and backing up. "Bad cat. Mother *fucker*. No! That's a bad fucking cat!"

But the cat kept stepping toward him, slowly, low to the ground, growling, ready to pounce. The cat looked either injured or sick. He was skinny, with a slightly awkward hitch, as if he had a barb in his foot, just right, where every now and then, he stepped on it. The hunting must have been worse with all the rain—and a bad leg.

"Oh, fuck," Gilbert said as the cat's hind end shifted and tail twitched once. Gilbert knew what was coming next. Snowball always shook his butt just like that right before he'd pounce. Gilbert tried to break this cat's train of thought, like he would with Snowball. "Hey!" he yelled suddenly, throwing his arms up to the left, thinking it would disrupt the cat's flow and timing.

But at Gilbert's first move, the cat attacked, flying through the air, his front legs and paws out in front of him, claws out, and his giant back legs snapping up from behind like a catapult, zeroing in on Gilbert's mid-section. He hit Gilbert with all four legs at once. Gilbert's arms were raised to try to protect his face, and the cat's back paws landed on the tarpaper kimono and the claws snapped out of their sheaths and tore through the tarpaper and sunk into Gilbert's belly. The front paws hit at the exact same moment in a flurry, and Gilbert dropped the knife. The back legs were a barbed rocket to the belly, pushing Gilbert backward as the front claws slashed and then dug in, one under Gilbert's right armpit and the other on his left shoulder, pulling back against the force of the back legs. The collision sent Gilbert smashing backwards to the ground with a whipping force as the claws on the cat's front paws tore through his skin in the opposite direction of the overall force, pulling Gilbert back like a rat trap. As the forward claws made it through all the purchase they had in Gilbert's skin, Gilbert's top half let loose and his head came whipping down on the ground behind the rest of him. There was an explosion in his head, and his vision immediately went black as he felt himself rolling off the four-foot ledge that had been behind him, the cat's claws reinserted into his ribs.

CHAPTER 48 | REAPER

GILBERT'S EYES SHIVERED awake, like a short-circuiting robot coming back on-line, and he reeled with an explosion of pain. Of it all, his head hurt the worst. He was severely concussed. But his brain was unable to ponder such frivolities at that time. As his swimming and undefined sight came and went from focus, his whole field of vision was engulfed with the rose-pink chin of the mountain lion, dripping with his own blood. The cat was lying on top of him, like Snowball would when he'd catch his little leather mouse.

The cat must have thought Gilbert was dead, and was covering him, while eyeing Trent.

As he came to, Gilbert could hear Trent yelling, and then an awful half-scream, half-howl. Gilbert was still in a daze, not fully comprehending where he even was in the split second between waking up and finding himself under a mountain lion. The burst of action and light and pain made Gilbert flinch as he came to, and he watched in a receding fog as the cat suddenly realized he wasn't dead. The cat's head snapped down, and then he and Gilbert were eye to eye for a nanosecond. The cat's pupils opened like an explosion of black fireworks, filling his eyes, and he whipped his head back and then down, and Gilbert watched his death descend on him in slow motion, the cat's head—ears back, eyes wide—firing into Gilbert's neck.

Gilbert didn't have time to respond, to physically move to fight. There was but that brief second that the cat recognized life, and they met each other's eyes. In real time, it was nothing, and the ensuing attack was a bullet. There was no reacting. But somehow, the brain has time in that split-second for a starburst of thought, a flash that comes all at once—and yet is linear and integrated and layered. He thought mostly of Jeannie. He thought of her going to his funeral. He thought of what that would do to the rest of her life. His dying. What would that do? It would be awful. He wished in that instant that he'd never gone on the camping trip. Why had he? What was he doing out on Santanoni Peak? Why was he even here? It was crazy. It was stupid. He had a warm house and a warm bed and a warm wife. He had work to do, and books to read, and a million other things that were higher on the priority list than a stupid trip anywhere with Trent, let alone out in the woods. *I'm going to die out here!* He kicked himself. *Why? Why, you idiot? Now you're dead! In the middle of the fucking woods in the middle of nothing!* It all seemed so stupid in that moment when it became clear it would result in death. The one death Gilbert had to give. There in the woods at the end of the fangs of a fucking cat—that didn't even exist in the Adirondacks. All for nothing. He wanted to cry. Why? Why had he done it?

CHAPTER 49 | FRIENDS

BEHIND THE SACRAMENT Marina on Lake George, Gilbert shivered as he sat in his car. *This is stupid. Go home,* he told himself and reached for the ignition. The little blue Toyota rattled to life, and he grabbed the gear shifter and yanked it down and punched the gas, swinging out into the road to return the way he'd arrived. He was flustered, suddenly scared and sweating on the cool night. Once you start running from some unknown thing in the dark, each second seems to take forever and make the thing more real. Concern becomes terror. He didn't feel like he would be able to breathe until he was off this back road and back to the relative comfort of the highway.

He took a deep breath and tried to calm his nerves, like he'd taught himself with poker. But as he swung the car around to return to the highway, his headlights swept across the road and down toward the marina warehouse. As the faded dual yellow cones of light flashed across the scene, five figures appeared out of the blackness. One was Jimmy Dove, one was Trent, two others were Jimmy's guys, and the fifth figure was dead and wrapped in heavy clear plastic, secured with duct tape. They were between an open warehouse door and the open back tailgate of Trent's Chevy Suburban—with the custom rims.

Gilbert balked at what he saw for that split second. A body? There were rumors that that was why Jimmy Dove owned part of that marina—and why he was so unreasonably respected by the higher-ups in the Bogacci family. The body would probably go out onto one of Jimmy's charter boats that night and be fish food by the morning, nourishing the giant, primordial northern pike and lake trout lurking in the depths of the ancient lake. The poor bastard's bones would mix on the bottom with other unfortunates throughout history: soldiers from the French and Indian War, drunken summer recreationists, and a long, steady stream of enemies of the Friends. Since the days of Lucky Luciano and the forming of the Commission of the Five Families, guys were sent "upstate." Gilbert had heard ice fishermen joke that they had John Gotti and Vito Genovese to thank for why they pulled record lake trout out of the lake.

But this was no joke around the stove in a cold, winter ice shanty. This was real, and he shouldn't have seen what he just saw.

As Gilbert's headlights flashed across the scene,

all four living faces snapped toward him in his little blue Toyota.

Immediately, they dropped the dead guy, and Trent jumped toward his Suburban, parked at an angle to block any sight of their deed from the quiet boats bobbing in the harbor beyond.

That was the last thing Gilbert saw at the marina. He punched the gas, and his little blue Toyota whipped around, and he took off up the road. The road was narrow, a small country road that mostly just ran to the back of the marina. He drove as fast as he could until he reached the main road that ran along the southern end of the lake, Bay Road. He squealed out into the lane, hoping like hell that no one was coming, gunning it toward town, watching his rearview.

Then he saw them: the first flashes of Trent's headlights behind him as he rounded the first bend on Bay Road.

"Shit!" he yelled, wishing he had a faster car, or a better head start.

The road ahead of him was dark and winding, barely wider than a bike path, running along the dark cliffs and heavy forest at the edge of the lake. The lake was a black void out in the distance, falling from below the road, offering no harbor or direction. But Gilbert gunned it for all his little blue Toyota was worth. He knew this road—he hoped.

Gilbert raced through the curves. He knew that

he would be just as dead as the poor bastard in the duct-tape diving suit if Trent and Jimmy Dove caught up to him. He had to hope that they hadn't gotten a good look at his car. It was dark and the trees were thick in that area. Maybe they hadn't seen it well.

But he knew that whether they had seen him before or not, *now* all they had to do was get close enough to recognize his car. If they did that, that was it, he was *D-E-D*, as Dean Martin would say. All they had to had to do was see his car.

He drove like death was riding up his ass. He encountered three other vehicles on that road: two coming at him and one going his way. All three were unhappy to see him rounding the bends in the middle of the road at eighty miles an hour.

A few miles later, at Beach Road, Gilbert swung a squealing right, passing on the left side of the two young lovers sitting in their car, quietly waiting at the stop sign onto Bay Road. They looked at him in terror as he swerved around them on the wrong side, skidding one of his back tires off the road before correcting behind their car and gunning it down Beach Road toward Lake George village.

When he reached the other cars full of families out for a cruise along the pier to look at the lake and the steamboats and the old colonial-era fort across the boardwalk, he slowed. Once he was nestled into the traffic, he would be safe—if they hadn't seen his car.

He drove a normal speed for the final half-mile before he pulled into one of a series of parking lots across from the boardwalk. He drove to the second row and pulled in slowly and turned off his lights and sat there, hoping not to see anything other than happy families out at the arcades and docks and mini-golf courses.

As he sat holding his breath, trying to slow his heart, trying to not move, his eyes dropped to the dash-cam sitting on his dash, flashing red for *record*, like it always did when the car was on.

CHAPTER 50 | DESCENDING

IN THE FOREST, facing the mountain lion, the explosion of thought blasting through Gilbert's head as he watched his death descend upon him was like the full dream in the seconds before waking. He watched the mountain lion's head snapping down and even thought about certain aspects: the size of the teeth, the perfect black, white, and gold coloring of the cat's face. But it was a flash, a terror in which he thought about his own demise, and the carrier of that death.

But in that same split-second, as he pondered the size of the teeth, a black shape came into view behind the cat and went flying over. It was Trent. He had managed to hop over to the knife and then to the short ledge to fling himself over, stabbing the cat in the back as he tackled it off of Gilbert and went rolling down the hill.

It came in an increment of time so small as to be nearly immeasurable before the teeth entered Gilbert's neck. The cat snapped around at the first sight of Trent flying over, and then Trent and the cat both went crashing down the rocky slope to the left of Gilbert.

Trent screamed and there was a sickening sound of the further evisceration of his broken leg. He crashed down and rolled, and the mountain lion rolled with him and eventually came out on top of Trent, much like he had with Gilbert just moments before, a knife wound now in his back.

The attack surprised the cat, and pissed it off, but didn't injure it seriously. Not seriously enough, and the lion snapped its head back and fired it down at Trent's neck just like it had at Gilbert's. But Trent was ready for it and had his arms free. He grabbed the mountain lion by the neck as the jaws came down and the two of them, Trent and the mountain lion, collided like two trains on one track and locked into each other, each baring his teeth and holding his foe by hands and claws. The lion sent a flurry of claws at Trent's head, body, and face, but Trent held firm and shook. The two struggled and thrashed and rolled over, and then Trent was on top. Trent pushed himself up with the force he was pushing down onto the mountain lion's windpipe, and he shook the cat and the cat thrashed and fought with every leg and claw in a final struggle for its life before the shivers that would precede his death. He was choking, gasping, the life draining from him, and Trent had an iron grip on his neck.

But in a last thrashing flurry before death, jerking in a spree of convulsions, the cat's head snapped around and one long, sharp fang just barely caught Trent's left arm.

But it was enough.

A smattering of blood flung into the air as the single tooth sliced through the flesh at the back of Trent's forearm. Trent howled and pulled back for a split second. But it loosened his grip on the cat's neck, which allowed a spirit of oxygen into the cat's lungs that traveled like a spark through the cat's muscles, and he sprang up and kicked all four legs into Trent's midsection, sending Trent rolling down the grade.

The cat flipped himself level and landed on all fours in the same motion as the kick, and was already in a gallop for the forest before he even touched ground, the bleeding knife wound causing an awkward limp to the frantic sprint.

CHAPTER 51 | SLIP

NEARLY THREE WEEKS after the car chase from the Sacrament Marina, Gilbert, Jeannie, Liz, and Trent sat in Jeannie and Liz's parents' back yard. It was a warm, early August night, and they'd been barbequing. Jeannie and Liz's parents were inside doing some of their evening rituals while the rest of them sat out back having an after-dinner drink.

For Trent and Liz, that drink came after a number of before-dinner and during-dinner drinks, too. They were starting to get into it, like they often would, when suddenly Gilbert heard Liz shout, "I already sent Gilbert to go find you at your whore's house up in Lake George a few weeks ago, you asshole!"

Gilbert never mentioned that night at the marina to anyone. It was the first time he could remember lying to his wife about anything other than whether he really wanted to go see the movie she wanted to see. When he got home that night, he told Jeannie—and she told Liz—

that he started to go find Trent but decided it wasn't right and turned around. Jeannie wasn't upset with him, and she didn't throw out the meatballs—and he never said another word about that night to anyone. He didn't know what to say even if he wanted to. He wasn't even sure what he saw, and with each passing day, he grew less and less sure. Intentionally, after viewing the dashcam video once, he'd slammed down his laptop screen and never watched it again, almost allowing himself to believe it didn't exist. That it could have been anything wrapped up in that plastic. Maybe his mind was playing tricks. Maybe it wasn't even Trent's headlights behind him on Bay Road.

His mind definitely had been out of whack that night—but to what degree?

Maybe it was hope that made him doubt what he knew. Maybe he thought that if he ignored it, it would fade away and never have happened. Fear leads to hope.

And then Liz said what she said—on an otherwise perfectly peaceful evening after a nice barbeque with family: "I already sent Gilbert to go find you at your whore's house up in Lake George a few weeks ago, you asshole!"

Gilbert froze and stared down at his beer.

"You *what?*" Trent said to Liz, then turned slowly to Gilbert.

Gilbert kept looking at his beer.

"What do you mean, you sent Gilbert to find me? When was this?"

"I didn't even go," Gilbert said, a little too quickly.

"When was this?" Trent said to Liz.

"Fuck you, Trent," Liz said.

"Real nice," Trent sneered, then turned to Gilbert. "When was this, Gilbert? Where'd you go? Why didn't you just call me?"

"Trent, drop it," Jeannie stepped in, leaning between Gilbert and Trent.

"I didn't even go," Gilbert said, putting a hand on Jeannie's shoulder, silently telling here he had it.

"Of course not, Gilly," Trent said with a smile. "I know you're smarter than that. That'd be dumb."

"I decided as soon as I got in the car that it was stupid and I went to Stubby's Hoagies instead."

"*What?*" Jeannie yelled and they all looked at her, surprised at her sudden outburst. "You got Stubby's and didn't bring me one?"

"It's not funny, Jeannie," Liz snapped at her sister.

"Don't start with me, Liz," Jeannie said with an authoritative finality. "This is between you and Trent. Gilbert did the right thing not going that night. You two need to figure this shit out without dragging us into it every time." And with that, she stood up and leaned over and gave her sister a quick kiss on the cheek. "Love you, babe."

"Love you, too," Liz said and pouted.

Gilbert stood and nodded to Trent who just nodded back with an unreadable grin.

CHAPTER 52 | WAVE

TRENT WAS BADLY injured. They were both torn to shreds.

"Trent?" Gilbert said. He was trying to sit up where the cat had left him, holding his head and wobbling to keep his balance even while lying down. "Trent," he said again, feebly. "Trent. Are you okay?"

Trent was lying on his back, down the slope. Gilbert could hear him groaning, gritting his teeth against the pain, but he could only see the bottom half of him from behind a rock. What he could see didn't look good. Trent's leg was in a bad direction again. The splint had come apart with the cat pulling on it, and the leap off the ledge and ensuing struggle had injured more than just the leg.

"Trent," Gilbert said again, barely more than a whisper, trying to sit up. He couldn't focus on anything, blinking his eyes harder and harder as if his internal mechanisms were just a little out of alignment, needing to be squeezed into place. But each time he opened his eyes, his vision was equally bad. He looked around, unsure of exactly where he was. He knew he was with Trent. There was a cat. He hit his head. He was alive—at least to the best of his knowledge. But his vision wouldn't get right, wouldn't come into alignment.

"Trent," he said, a little louder, but then had to lie down again because he was about to puke. His head was throbbing.

He took some breaths and the nausea subsided and he lay there, feeling an odd warmth traveling up from his feet, a feeling as if lying down right there for a while would be a good idea. *Just a little while*, he thought as he drifted in and out of consciousness. He felt the warmth rushing now like an ocean wave that had suddenly hit the reef below the surface and then came driving up to the top half of his body and out the crown of his head in a flash.

And then he was unconscious.

CHAPTER 53 | INTENT

IT WAS TWO weeks after the barbeque that Liz supposedly came up with the idea that Gilbert and Trent should go on a camping trip. Jeannie thought it was a great idea, and Gilbert wanted to tell her the truth about it all, and didn't want to go in the least. But knowledge was a deadly poison in this scenario. She was only safe if she didn't know anything about what he saw, or what he thought he saw.

He told her he didn't want to go. She didn't push him, but she said it would be good for him, and joked with him about being a shut-in. He could tell she wanted desperately for everything to turn out roses, for them to all be a happy family. He knew she wanted it for Liz: to have a good partner, for them all to go out to dinner together.

He knew it would never happen. Not with Trent. Not now. But he couldn't tell her the truth. She couldn't know.

And he didn't even know if there was anything to know. He couldn't say for certain that Trent suspected anything at all about that night at the marina—or that he might come up with any kind of devious plan for the camping trip. But again, he had to play the range, and he knew that for Trent or anyone else, a camping trip is a pretty good time to shut someone up who might know something he shouldn't.

Of course, Gilbert wouldn't be hard to kill any day of the week. But a camping trip would make it easy.

The night before he left, Gilbert packed the gun that Jeannie didn't even know he had. He kept it for the same reason most people kept guns: he didn't know how to defend himself otherwise. A gun was a get-out-of-shit-alive card for someone like Gilbert—he hoped. It was the only thing that made him feel like he could protect Jeannie. Late on that last night home, he uncovered it in its place in the closet and packed it into the right side pocket of his camping pack, hidden, but accessible, he reasoned.

In the end, it was a terrible place to pack it. When he had fallen into the lake trying to net the fish on the first day, it had either fallen out of the pocket and sunk to the bottom of the lake, or Trent had found it and taken it as he gathered their bags in the commotion. Either way, it was a stupid place for it, and either way, it was sitting underwater, maybe by itself below where he tipped the boat, or maybe in with Trent's things, washed down from their lean-to on Cold River.

Gilbert looked over at Trent as they shuffled along the trail. Still to that moment he didn't know if

Trent ever intended to kill him—or if he intended to kill him still. He may already have killed him, of course, with the wound on his side. Gilbert could be a dead man walking. He didn't know.

But the more he thought about Trent's motives—and maybe it was a delusion drawn from hope—he started to think that maybe it was just giant bags of illegal cigarettes or something like that that they were loading out of Trent's Suburban that night at the marina. Maybe they were just clearing out some storage space. Deep down he knew it was Trent and Jimmy Dove and two other non-saints dumping a body, but he could still cast doubt in his own mind. The easiest thing to believe is what you want to believe. The easiest mark is yourself. So, Gilbert leaned into those thoughts, and by the time he was stepping into that canoe at the Long Lake public boat launch, he was almost convinced that Trent wasn't planning to kill him out there in the woods.

CHAPTER 54 | CONSCIOUS

GILBERT AWOKE TO Buck yelling at him from up on the ledge above them.

"Buck," Gilbert croaked, raising his arm up toward him.

Buck gestured for him to wait and then disappeared, making his way down the path to their level.

Then Gilbert heard Trent below him and turned.

"Gilbert. Oh, God, Gilbert. Wake up."

Gilbert shook his head and it felt like some kind of science experiment in his skull, an expanding, hard foam—made of razor blades—squeezing his head from the inside out, growing larger and larger, and pressing more and more with every move he made. It felt like it was choking him. Not that it was in his neck, but that he for some reason couldn't breathe because of it, like the growing razor foam was taking up any extra space in his body and there wasn't any room left for air in his lungs or even the blood pumping in his chest. Each beat of his heart drove the razors out from the foam in all directions and a million swords into the pit of his skull.

"Gilbert. Shit. Gilbert, wake up," Trent was moaning on the slope below him.

Gilbert could still only see the lower half of Trent's legs, and Trent couldn't see him.

"Gilbert," Trent moaned again. It was a good amount later in the day, probably mid-afternoon. "Gilbert. Gilbert, wake up," Trent kept muttering, tears and physical pain thick in his voice.

Gilbert could hear him, but couldn't bring himself to speak. He still couldn't bring himself to even breathe. What breaths came were weak and involuntary. "Buck," he tried to say.

"Gilbert?" Trent yelped from below at the sound.

"Trent," Gilbert managed to squeak out.

"Gilbert!" Trent screeched, flopping around behind the rock that blocked their sight of each other.

"Trent," Gilbert said. "Buck is—"

"Gilbert!"

"Trent. Buck—"

"Gilbert! Gilbert! You're alive!"

Gilbert had to take a breath. He lay there.

"Gilbert. Gilbert, are you okay? Gilbert. Are you okay? I can't fucking see you. *Dammit!*"

"Trent," Gilbert managed to say. "Trent." Then a pause. "Buck is—"

"Gilbert. Gilbert, what are you saying? Gilbert. I can't hear you. Is the cat gone?"

"Buck—"

"Gilbert. What are you saying? Gilbert! Are you alive?"

But Gilbert was already unconscious.

CHAPTER 55 | MOVING

GILBERT CAME TO with a light rain sprinkling his face. The clouds and the sky had darkened. It was well into dusk. He was freezing cold and immediately started shivering violently. The shivers raked shards of glass around the inside of his head. But while the pain was debilitating, his head was fractionally better than when he woke earlier. He could hear Trent below in a monotonous moaning croak. "Gilbert— Gilbert," he said, over and over, with a "wake up," every now and then.

Gilbert shivered and held his head and rolled on his side and pulled his knees into his chest, hugging them—lightly, because strain hurt—trying for some kind of warmth and something to ease his nauseated stomach. As he lay curled on his side, he saw a small pile of stones beside him—a cairn just like the ones Buck had been making in the lean-to the first morning they met.

He's gone for help, Gilbert thought, allowing hope to creep in, if only for a second. He rolled onto his back and took a deep breath and let it out, then breathed in again and called out to Trent with all he could muster. "Trent!" he said, and it came out like the death rattle of a skewered frog.

"Gilbert!" Trent shouted in a raspy voice. "Gilbert!"

"I'm here, Trent," Gilbert said, lying on his back. "I'm here."

"Gilbert, that cat has been back around. Oh, God, Gilbert. I'm so glad you're alive."

"Are you okay?"

"I don't know. I can't move from the pain. My leg is bad. I don't even want to look at it."

"Just give me a minute to see if I can stand up."

"That cat's around, Gilbert. Watch yourself. Oh, God, I thought he might have been up there eating your dead body. Oh, man, I'm so glad you're alive."

"When did you last see him?"

"Not too long ago. Fifteen, twenty minutes maybe."

"Shit," Gilbert said and held his pulsing head.

"Can you move?"

"I haven't tried yet. But I think I can." And with that he slowly rose to a sitting position. His vision was clearer than before, but his head was still throbbing. "I'm sitting up and it feels okay," he announced down to Trent.

"Just watch your back."

Gilbert slowly swung his legs to the downhill side

of himself and found a level spot to place them and try to stand up. He scooched himself into position and gave it a half-a-try. The brief swing up to almost-standing and then back down again didn't do his head any favors, but was bearable. On the next push, he made it all the way to his feet and stood for a long ten seconds before wavering slightly and deciding to sit back down. It was only discomfort, though. He believed he could manage.

"I think I can stand," he said down to Trent.

"Just take it slow."

Gilbert rose to his feet, and held his hands out for balance, and before long he felt fairly stable. With his eyes blinking forcefully, Gilbert picked his way down the hill to Trent.

"Oh, God, you're a sight for sore eyes," Trent said when Gilbert came around the rock, arms out like Frankenstein.

Gilbert made it to the rock next to Trent and sat down. His head hurt, but his balance was still mostly intact. He felt like he could walk. But for now, he had the unenviable task of checking Trent's substantial injuries. He gathered his focus and shivered at the sight of Trent's leg: broken and chewed and broken again and left out in the rain. It was ugly. But the worst news for them was the other leg, the other foot. The ankle was badly sprained from the fall. It was impossible to tell if it was broken, but with his other leg in the shape it was, it would be difficult for them to carry on like they had before.

"I need to go for help," Gilbert said, unconvincingly. "I think we're close enough now."

"No. If you leave me out here, I'm dead. You know that. That cat is out here."

Gilbert looked down at the ground and palmed his hair forward silently.

Trent propped himself up and took a deep breath. "Just— We're both alive. We can do this."

"We better hope Buck is sending help," Gilbert said, looking off.

"What?"

"He came by while I was knocked out. I saw him. And he left a pile of rocks right by me to let me know he was going for help."

"A pile of rocks?"

"A cairn."

"And that was *Buck* telling you that he was going for help?"

"Yeah," he said and shook his head, confused. "You didn't believe me about the cat either." He rubbed at his eyes, trying to make it all clear. "He was doing it before. And he said he'd leave me a sign."

"He said that just now?"

"Before."

"Why didn't he write you a note?"

"A note? You got a fucking pen and paper, Trent?"

"It just doesn't make sense. Why didn't he come down to me?"

"You didn't believe me about the cat either," he repeated, "and now look at us.

Trent just raised his eyebrows, conceding the point.

"He went for help," Gilbert muttered, rubbing his head.

"Okay, Gilbert," Trent said, eyeing him. "Either way, if you leave me out here, that cat will have me for dinner before you're out of sight. And then come for you after that, too, probably. The only chance we have is to stay together."

Gilbert just looked at him and frowned.

"I saved your fucking life, Gilbert," Trent said.

Gilbert just looked at him for a long time. "You may have killed me, too, Trent," he said, holding his side where the ever-worsening wound hid under a bandage and a tarpaper kimono.

"Gilbert. I was out of my mind."

"Were you?"

"What does that mean?"

"You know exactly what it fucking means." The exclamation made him lightheaded, and he swayed, almost passing out.

"What do you mean, *I know exactly what it means?*" Trent said, eyeing him.

"What was this camping trip about for you, Trent?"

"What?"

Gilbert just gave him an accusatory stare.

"You sound crazy, Gilbert."

"No, I don't, and you know it."

"I don't know what the hell you're talking about. We just had some bad luck on a camping trip, Gilbert, and we need to help each other to get out."

Gilbert squinted his eyes, trying to decide if he believed anything Trent was saying.

But he didn't know what to believe. His head was muddled with pain, hunger, loss of blood, and concussion—maybe fever and infection, too. He was having a hard time even remembering his name. Had he even seen Trent at the marina? Yes. Yes. He had a video. But, was that from a movie? He didn't know about anything anymore.

"We just need to get to that lake, Gilbert. It's not far."

"Can you even move?"

"Not where I am right now. But if you pull me out of here and splint this leg again, I think I can keep moving.

Gilbert found the torn tarpaper splint up above them and reused it. Before long, they had Trent's leg redressed and his other boot tightened around the sprain. With his crutch and Gilbert to help steady him, they could move similarly to before, just slower and with more pain.

Gilbert's head still ached and the new cuts and scratches from the mountain lion lay open and bleeding.

They hadn't seen the mountain lion since Gilbert woke up, but that didn't mean it wasn't out there. By all accounts, it had hidden itself from everyone in the Adirondacks for as long as it had been alive. It was a good place to hide, with areas nearby that no human had ever stepped, where an animal could live undetected for years. Where the only law was nature. *Here be monsters*, said the old maps. *Avoid at all costs, ye of light heart.*

"To the lake. To the lake," Trent kept saying under his breath with each step, like a mantra.

"Do you think mountain lions have been here all along, just staying out of sight?" Gilbert asked.

"Maybe a pet?" Trent said then paused, looking over at Gilbert. "You were right, Gilbert. It really was a mountain lion."

Gilbert rolled his eyes, but it was Trent's way of saying sorry, and he took it for what it was worth.

Gilbert shrugged. "I hate thinking it could be out there, stalking us."

"Then don't."

Gilbert nodded and frowned and they kept moving.

"To the lake. To the lake," Trent muttered as they went.

CHAPTER 56 | FLASH

THEY REACHED THE lake in the middle of the night. The grade was gentler as they approached, and they found a herd path that eventually led right to the lake.

The moon was bright behind the cloud cover, and it lit the sky, but the clouds held rank, and the rain still fell in a light drizzle that danced along the calm surface of the water. Both directions around were blocked, one by fast-moving water and one by a rising swamp. Halfway across the lake in the most direct heading to the safety of the highway was a series of large islands. They both agreed that the size of one of the islands made the open distances from the shore to the island and the island to the shore on the other side short enough to believe that with some kind of float to hold onto for the deeper crossing, they could make it across the lake. It was their last obstacle. On the other side: a road and the outer houses of the Town of Newcomb.

By the time they reached the lake, they were a

huddled ball, teetering through the forest, holding onto each other, falling and supporting together and simultaneously. It was around midnight, thirteen days after Gilbert had paced the dock of the Long Lake public boat launch, watching with growing dread as Trent packed their gear into the canoe at the beginning of the trip. Now, Gilbert looked down at himself and at Trent as they limped through the mud, bloody and broken and starving and missing parts of themselves, and he couldn't believe what he saw. It was then that the conscious realization of the depths of his decent, what his survival had cost, what he had become, what he had been reduced to, what parts of him were lost or destroyed, what madness had taken hold, suddenly arrived. And when his diminished mind struck that awful thought, pulled as tight as a piano string, pain flashed from every wound on his body.

CHAPTER 57 | SPREAD

THEY DECIDED TO rest at the edge of the water, to gain strength for their crossing. Gilbert helped Trent to the ground beside a tree and then sat down gingerly behind him, his head ringing. He closed his eyes and squinted them until the ringing lightened to a manageable level. Then he opened his eyes just a sliver and stared at Trent, sitting, facing away from him.

"That cat's gonna come back," Trent said, drained and slumped against the tree. "We can't stop moving."

Gilbert just stared at the back of Trent's head, an anger rising like the fever inside him. "I'm going to die out here," he said.

"Don't say that, Gilbert," Trent said, turning back toward him. "We're not far. We just have to cross this lake and we won't be far."

"I can feel it inside that cut on my side," Gilbert said. "The fucking stab wound, Trent. Where you stabbed me."

"Gilbert."

"You did, Trent."

"I was out of my head."

"No, you weren't."

"Yes, I was, Gilbert."

"No, you *weren't!*" Gilbert shouted, and then his head rang like a bell. He squinted his eyes and grabbed his head to make it stop.

"You're gonna hurt yourself, Gilbert. You're acting crazy."

The bell subsided and Gilbert focused again on Trent. "I'm dying, Trent. You killed me."

"No, I didn't, Gilbert."

"Yes, you *did.*"

"No, I *didn't*—and now is not the time for this."

"This is the perfect time for this, Trent. I'm about to die out here. I need to know why you killed me."

"I didn't kill you, Gilbert!" he seethed. "You're gonna be fine. We just need to get across this lake and stay focused. We can find help."

"You killed me, Trent." The momentary zest had drained from Gilbert, and he just stared back at Trent, his eyes drooping as the jackhammer in his head commenced its concerto. He held his head and slumped to the ground.

He was only out for a second, but it felt like he was swimming out of the depths of a swamp, everything murky and out of focus.

When he came to, Trent was turned and looking

down at him. They were still sitting in the cluster of trees by the lake. Gilbert jerked awake with a start.

"Gilbert?" Trent said. "Are you okay?"

"We need to get to help," Gilbert said, his voice trembling. "We need to— to get help."

"We just need to get across this lake and we'll be close, Gilbert. We can do this."

"My fucking head is ringing," Gilbert said. "Just give me a minute." He held his head and moaned, but nothing made it better.

CHAPTER 58 | CROSS

THE FIRST LEG of the crossing, to the island in the middle of the lake, wasn't bad. The water was only four feet deep at its deepest, so they were able to wade across, mostly, without issue.

On the island, Gilbert gathered three small logs between blazing strikes of headache. With the logs arranged as a raft, they began to swim across the wider, deeper section from the island to the land on the other side.

The slight resistance of the water against Trent's bad leg made him scream in pain, and more than once, he almost lost his grip of the raft. The last time Trent lost his grip, his head slid all the way under the surface as the pain shut him down. As it happened, Gilbert watched for just an extra split second. He watched as Trent's feeble screams peaked and his eyes rolled back and he slipped slowly from the three logs, being pulled to the gravitational center of the earth, far beyond the floor of the lake, deep into the darkness grasping at their feet and the unknown below, where we will all one day return.

It was only a moment, only long enough for the water to go from Trent's chin to the top of his head. But in that moment, Gilbert had another flurry of thought, again more than the time could allow. He thought about Snowball, his cat. He thought about second grade. He thought about the Eagles—the band, for some reason. He thought about everything in his life, it seemed. He thought about murder. The word. The action. The intent? He didn't know.

The cold, dark waters slid from Trent's neck to his ears to the top of his skull—and Gilbert watched.

But before Trent's arms slipped into the water with the rest of him, Gilbert finally reached down and snagged him and pulled him up enough that he awoke from his pain-induced unconsciousness, still half submerged.

Gilbert watched as Trent came to under the water and struggled and tried to scream. But in those first moments of realization, his body tried to suck in a breath to scream with, and in rushed the waters of Newcomb Lake. Luckily for him, his instinctual convulsion was to pull himself up, and with Gilbert's help, he rose above the surface with his lungs spewing out the water they had just received.

He coughed and shook and spit, screaming in pain every time he moved. But Gilbert held him onto the makeshift raft and kicked them the rest of the way to the shore.

CHAPTER 59 | FEAR

GILBERT PUSHED THE Thai noodles around on his plate. They were at the Saratoga Mall food court and Jeannie was looking across the table at him, smiling like she always did.

"You're not going to go?"

"I don't think so," Gilbert said.

"Why not?"

"I don't know. I just don't want to."

Jeannie eyed him.

"It's just not worth it," he continued. "It's a small game. I'm not feeling lucky." As he spoke, he looked past Jeannie, and then to the left and the right, and finally, fighting the urge as long as he could, behind him. Every way he looked, he saw *associates*, goons, and they always seemed to be looking at him.

In reality, the big, bad, mob goon in the corner was probably just an insurance salesman, and the one behind the counter of Auntie Anne's pretzels was probably just the owner of Auntie Anne's pretzels. But why was he in a suit? Was he just checking the register? Or would he follow Gilbert into the restroom and cinch a Russian garrote around his neck?

"Gilbert!" Jeannie yelled for the third time before he snapped out of it. "What is up with you?"

"What?"

"What's up with you, Gilbert?"

"What? No. I'm just. Sorry. Sorry. I'm just a little distracted."

"You haven't wanted to do anything lately. I had to twist your arm to come here."

"It's the mall," Gilbert said, holding his hands palms up.

Jeannie conceded the point, but it didn't alleviate her concern. "What's up, Gubby? Seriously?"

"No, I'm fine," Gilbert said, shaking his head, unconvincingly.

"You need to play some poker. You should go."

"I know, I know," Gilbert said and palmed his hair forward.

"And I've got some terrible chick flicks that I need to watch."

Gilbert smirked at Jeannie, and she smiled back at him. There was nothing else in the world to him when she smiled. It all disappeared. All his anxieties were gone—but for the greatest anxiety of all, of course: love. Her face was so loving and warm. She complained about her cheeks growing chubby, but Gilbert couldn't get enough. She was so kind and caring and better than Gilbert in every way. People smiled at her, random people. And she smiled back. She had that thing that everyone can sense, in a sixth-sense kind of way. She exuded love and warmth and understanding. She was everything that was good with the world. She was a shining light that would help save the world from the darkness forever closing in. She was the only hope of humanity. With people like Jeannie, the evil could never win.

And it was for people like Gilbert to shield this shining light from the darkness. It was up to him to protect this goodness in the world. It was up to him. He must be the cannon fire at the gates.

CHAPTER 60 | ROAD

THEY BROKE THROUGH the brush and fell out into the middle of a road. It wasn't much of a road, barely as wide as a car and made of dirt. But it was a road. There would be houses on it.

They were close.

On the road, they made their way slowly, barely better than they had in the woods. The rain had increased again and the road was muddy and there was a gurgling stream that had formed and was running down the side where it would normally be dry. Each step sloshed in the muddied gravel of the deteriorating road.

After a long time, what felt like forever, traveling the muddy lane, they finally came around a bend and saw a house and another building standing there like holy angels. They were beautiful, made of carefully crafted wooden walls resting on ornate mortar and fieldstone foundations. The lawns were well-tended and the properties blended beautifully into the Adirondack forest, nature and home living hand in hand. Gilbert dropped to his knees and started crying when he saw the house. It was only a hundred yards away. They were saved.

Trent wobbled above him on the thick branch he was using as a crutch. "Holy shit," he said, staring at the house as if to make sure it was real.

Gilbert almost couldn't believe it.

His first thought was of Jeannie. He would see Jeannie again. She would nurse him back to health. She would cook him chicken soup and drive him to the doctor. She would rub his head while he vegged on the couch, recovering from his camping trip, his attempt at heroism—or whatever this was.

But just as he was having these thoughts, just as he knew he was saved, he heard a scuffling slosh in the mud behind him and looked back just in time to react ever so slightly as Trent swung his heavy crutch-branch down at Gilbert's head. Gilbert's slight ducking was just enough to deflect the blow—maybe to save his life. It still hurt like hell, and he lost himself for a moment, but it didn't knock him out.

In swinging his weapon, Trent lost balance and went to the ground. As he did, he continued swinging the branch wildly, trying to connect with Gilbert's head. He landed a couple of glancing shots on his way down, but no direct hits to anywhere that mattered, and when he hit the ground, he was momentarily incapacitated with pain. He howled.

Gilbert regained his senses and was suddenly alert, his last reserves of adrenaline brought forth by the shock of the sneak attack. He lunged up from all fours onto Trent who had just hit the ground, howling from the pain after his failed assault. Gilbert landed on him, trying to place his knee into Trent's bad leg. It worked. It wasn't a direct shot, but it was enough, landing to another howl of pain blasting out of Trent.

The momentary distraction of intense pain was just enough for Gilbert to gain the upper hand. They struggled, but Gilbert had a good hold on Trent's right arm and had him pulled onto his side so his left arm was pinned under him and useless. As long as that arm stayed under, Gilbert had a chance. Normally, Trent was much stronger than Gilbert, and he kept himself in shape, and was experienced in fighting. Gilbert would be no match for him if they stood hale and hearty, face to face. But Trent was badly injured and Gilbert was on top of him in the mud, grinding his knee into the compound fracture on Trent's left leg, sending Trent's howls out across the puddles of the road.

Gilbert concentrated on keeping hold of the one arm, the right arm, with both of his hands and arms and his body. He remembered his cousin Edmund holding the steers so the cowboys could administer medicine on his family's ranch out west in Wyoming. Gilbert and Jeannie had gone out there to visit a few years ago on a trip to Grand Teton and Yellowstone National Parks. Edmund and the family showed them around, and Gilbert and Jeannie got to watch them do some of their work on the ranch, which that day involved treating a sick steer out in the field.

After the cowboys had roped the steer to the ground, Edmund—an eager twenty-year-old eastern city transplant who spent his school year studying science in Manhattan and his summers in Wyoming—jumped down off his horse and leapt with a yelp on top of the thousand-pound steer as the cowboys held the steer with their ropes around his head and back legs. Edmund flopped down on that bucking and struggling steer and got hold of one of the front legs and bent it back on itself so the steer couldn't get it out in front of him to get upright and try to run or fight.

Then came the dangerous part. Once Edmund had that front leg folded back on itself, he gave a sign to the cowboy who had the head roped. At that time, with Edmund pinning the steer to the ground, with his weight and his grip on the one bent front leg the only thing keeping him from getting tossed and trampled, the cowboy loosened the rope he had around the steer's head, freeing the giant shoulders and head of the beast to thrash and ram. Then it was just Edmund and that big snorting steer, frothing at the mouth with giant black eyes rolling back and forth in his head.

For the next five seconds, Edmund was on his own for the front half of that animal. With the one front leg pinned, he had to use his own weight to keep the steer on its side. Then he had to use his one free hand to grab the rope from around the steer's neck, get the steer's head up off the ground for clearance, pull the rope off of the head, and quickly slip the loop around the first, loose leg. And then, finally, in a sleight-of-hand maneuver with the highest consequences, he had to slip the loop over the bent leg he was holding, having to let it loose to get the rope on, but still hold it firm until the loop finally found its groove with the two front legs crossed over one another at what would be the wrist.

Then, provided he'd done all of this correctly, the cowboy snapped the rope taut in a flash and looped it around his saddle horn as his well-trained horse recognized the precise instant to pull back, fully ensnaring the writhing steer on the ground, front legs one way, back legs the other. Secure.

That's what Gilbert thought of as he held onto Trent's arm and pressed all of his weight down, trying to stay as centered as possible while still driving his knee into the injury. He took hold of Trent's arm just like his cousin Edmund had with that giant steer out in Wyoming, and he laid his weight on him and held on for dear life, Trent still on his side. Trent struggled and Gilbert fought to hold him down, and after a good connection with his knee to Trent's injury, Gilbert was able to twist Trent's arm around and behind him, pushing Trent face down.

They were near the edge of the dirt road, and

Trent's head swung around in a flurry from just above the outer edges of the stream of storm water running down the side of the road. Gilbert yanked Trent's arm until he howled, then pushed his face down. Trent resisted, but Gilbert held him fast, with all his weight on him. Gilbert took a strong hold on Trent's bent arm, as best he could with one hand, and freed his other hand up. He pinned Trent's arm and quickly flashed his other hand up to the back of Trent's head and repositioned, pushing down on Trent's neck with all the strength he could muster.

Trent shook and snapped his head back and forth, holding his face above the water for a few tense seconds, but eventually, Gilbert's weight was too much for Trent's neck to hold and his face smashed down into the two inches of runoff, grinding into the gravel below.

Gilbert held him there with all his strength.

Gilbert's eyes swam with the explosion of action and fatigue. He pressed himself down on Trent, gripping Trent's wrist and twisting his arm while mashing his face down into the gravel below the surface of the dirty brown water that was now flowing around his face. Trent struggled and flailed and kicked his one good leg back and forth, but Gilbert had him pinned, and after a final knee to his injury and a final flail, Gilbert saw the bubble pop out downstream as Trent took that last deadly breath of dirty water. With a final shudder, Trent was dead, drowned, lying eerily still across the road with only his face reaching the current of the sandy, run-off stream.

Gilbert rolled off Trent and lay there on his back, the hair on the back of his head hanging in the same stream he'd just used to kill Trent. Gilbert struggled to regain his breath, looking up at the sky.

He had just killed a man.

CHAPTER 61 | NET

GILBERT SAT AT his desk and wrote on a notepad. He stopped while he was writing and hung his head for a moment, uncertainty washing over him. He looked down into the camping pack and the .357 snub-nose revolver in the opened right-side pocket. Beside the pack were the other items he was bringing for the trip. None so important as that one.

"Know that I will only act if I am one hundred percent sure," he wrote. "I do not have an interest in fighting the mob, but if Trent knows that I have that video, then we have no choice but to protect ourselves. I hope to God that I'm wrong, Jeannie. I hope I'm wrong about it all. But I have to know. We can't look over our shoulders forever. I can't worry that they might kill you trying to get to me. So, I take this camping trip with my eyes wide open, to draw him out. I will find out for sure by offering him the opportunity. I'll play the cards I have, hoping I'm the fox and not the hare. Maybe it's crazy. But it's the only plan I could think of that had any possible outcome that we could live with, however difficult or improbable it might be." He paused for a long moment as he wrote.

"If you are reading this," he continued to write, "then I was not successful. I'm sorry, Jeannie. I really hope you don't get this." He hung his head as he was writing. "If you do, then be careful. The police and media will be getting the video as well. They'll get all they need. They don't need anything from you, so lock the door and don't trust or even talk to anyone, including the police. These are not nice guys. With me dead, I hope they'll be satisfied." He stopped and read the last sentence again, shivering. He knew what this would do to her. "I've hated having to lie to you. You know I can't keep anything from you. You're my everything. You're who I tell. But I hope you understand why I had to." His hands were shaking, and he dropped his head. No amount of wishing would get him out of this. "You and Liz and your parents need to get away from here for a little while," he wrote. "Hopefully just until it blows over. But you have to get away." He finished the letter through tears, worried for what might come.

In emails and envelopes to the FBI and seventeen news outlets, set to send automatically if he didn't return from his camping trip, with the dashcam video from that night at the marina attached, he wrote, "If you are receiving this, it's because I'm dead, killed to prevent you from seeing this video. In this case, I am your witness and your next victim. You can find my body somewhere around Long Lake in the town of Newcomb. I walk out into the wild right now willing to give my life for this. Do not let it be in vain."

CHAPTER 62 | VANISHING

GILBERT LAY ACROSS the road where he'd rolled off Trent's lifeless body, catching his breath and looking up at the big gray sky moving overhead. The sky did not care. It made no note of what had just transpired below it. It only rolled over, dark and gray. The fight took the last of whatever energy Gilbert had left. He breathed as deeply as he could, but he couldn't catch his breath. His muscles wouldn't chase out the weakness. As his blood slowed after the fight, it felt like the blood had turned to sludge, hardening in his vessels. To even raise his hand felt like more effort than he'd ever exerted on anything. It wasn't painful—in fact, the opposite. He felt like his blood was turning his body into a lifeless object, from the tips of his fingers and toes and up his arms and legs, all going numb in turn, a trickling tide of warmth and calmness and letting go, his body hardening into carbon, returning to the earth.

He suddenly shook his head, the idea of death wakening him from its comforting slumber like an electric shock. He shook his head again and shook his shoulders and what he could of his body until the blood returned to its living liquid form and ran again to the far reaches of its circuit.

Gilbert coughed and moaned and rolled himself over onto his side. From this horizontal position, he watched the muddy stream run down the road away from him. He looked up at the house back in the trees, only a hundred yards away. Had they not heard the struggle? Trent had screamed. It was late at night. But no light had come on.

Gilbert rolled himself onto his stomach and pulled himself across the ground toward the house. Every inch took incredible effort, but as he moved, the idea of rescue enlivened him just enough to keep him going. He was able to get to his hands and knees. His head felt like it would pop and his whole left side felt like it was poisoning him from the inside, trying to cut him in half, but he crawled until he reached the gravel driveway. He was only able to make one hand or knee move at a time, one, two, three, four, one, two, three, four.

He wobbled and fell at the foot of the driveway, not moving for a long time. His mind was swimming, dipping in and out of consciousness as he lay dying, half on the driveway and half in the road.

The thought of getting up, of not dying, of surviving, swam upstream through his drifting consciousness, running against a current that said to sleep, to rest, to die there, steps from salvation. That struggling thought fired its flares into the darkening sky of his mind and Gilbert pushed against the ground as hard as he could, pressing his shoulders up off the ground so he could see the house. Still no light. No one inside knew he was out there.

He moaned and turned his head toward the forest, slowly, and as he did, he looked back to where Trent was lying on the side of the road. Dead.

But his heart suddenly jumped.

Trent wasn't there.

For a sudden, terrifying moment, Gilbert thought Trent was standing over him about to drive a sharpened stick through the back of his skull. He dropped to his stomach on the ground and looked around himself in every direction, nausea rising.

At first, he didn't see anything.

He squirmed and spun around. Trent was out there somewhere. Where? The unknown spun his mind into craziness. He heard attacks coming from every direction. Every plop of a raindrop was the plop of footsteps running at him, always from the direction he wasn't looking.

Then, off in the woods, he saw a flash of Trent's shirt.

At first, Gilbert thought Trent was crawling through the woods, maybe sneaking, maybe flanking him. He moved so awkwardly. Then he thought maybe Trent was making a run for the house. He seemed to be crawling in that direction.

Between rapid blinks to clear his vision, Gilbert suddenly saw a swath of tan—and then the black-tipped ears, and finally the giant flashing green eyes of the mountain lion. He had Trent by the shoulder and was dragging his dead carcass out into the forest.

The confusion, and then the sight of a mountain lion dragging a dead human, pumped Gilbert's sludgy blood, and he made a crawling, scrambling dash across the wooded front yard of the house toward the front door and salvation.

CHAPTER 63 | GENESIS

GILBERT WALKED UP the short path to Liz's front door and knocked.

"Shit," he muttered to himself. He looked all around himself for the seventh time since he'd parked his little blue Toyota up the street from Liz's house. It was a hot, early August afternoon, a week after the night of the barbeque and three weeks before the canoe trip. He was sweating, bad—stress sweating. He smelled. Like old cabbage. He palmed his hair forward a few times, then took a series of long deep breaths, getting his heart rate under control.

He didn't know why he was so nervous. He knew why he was scared. He had been scared since he saw Trent and Jimmy Dove doing whatever they were doing with that body. But he felt nervous. Nervous because he hated lying. Bluffing at poker was one thing. But this wasn't poker. And this wasn't a bluff. Not quite.

"Gilbert?" Liz said as she opened the door and saw him. Then her face turned to horror as she saw his worried face. "Did something happen to Jeannie?"

"No, no," Gilbert said, holding his hands up— thrown off. "I just— I just wanted to talk for a second."

She gave him an odd look, but opened the door.

Liz guided him into the living room and motioned for him to sit down, flopping into a plush armchair herself, pinching the bridge of her nose.

Gilbert sat on the couch, only using the outer inches of the seat. His knees pointed toward the kitchen, opposite of Liz. His eyes studied the carpet.

"Jesus, Gilbert," Liz said with a grin. "Relax."

"Yeah," Gilbert said, and stayed how he was. "Sorry, I just— I—"

Liz's grin softened into a loving smile. "What is it, Gilbert?"

"I just want to make sure you're okay."

"Did Jeannie ask you to come over?"

The thought hadn't occurred to Gilbert. "No," he said. "This is just me."

"You're worried about Trent?"

"I just—" He paused.

"I know, Gilbert."

"But do you, Liz?"

"He's not the best guy to the outside world. But he's good to me." Her eyes slid to the floor as she said the last bit.

Gilbert peeked over at Liz as her eyes fell, and when her eyes rose again, his dropped to the floor in their place. "I know, Liz. I know."

Liz sighed and stood up. "You want something to drink? Water? Coffee? Vodka?"

Gilbert shrugged and nodded.

"Vodka it is then," she said, walking out into the kitchen.

Gilbert looked around, then stood up and followed Liz into the kitchen. As he passed the hallway on the left, he pointed to a large, outdoor backpack hanging from a hook on the wall. "Trent really likes to camp, huh?" he said, gesturing at the backpack and the other outdoor gear around the house.

Liz smiled, seeming happy for the change of subject. "Yeah, he goes out quite a bit," she said. "Beats his chest and rolls around in his own stink for a while. He likes it."

"I've never been," Gilbert said, glancing in her direction, hoping she'd take the bait, and hating himself for it.

"You haven't?" she said over her shoulder, surprised. She pulled two tall, skinny glasses from the upper cabinet and set them on the counter in front of her. "He took me a few times when we first met, when I was first trying to impress him. You're not missing much." She poured them both a short glass of vodka and then clinked Gilbert's as she handed it to him.

Gilbert nodded and took the glass and didn't say anything. He knew the best way to get someone to speak is to not say anything at all. Whether it's around a poker table or out in life, people hate an empty pause and will go out of their way to fill one. Gilbert was a walking empty pause. Which made him great at poker, but bad at small talk, and good at the deception currently underway.

As he was hoping, Liz carried on, talking about their camping trips until finally she stopped as if a great idea had occurred to her. She turned to him and said, "You and Trent should go camping! Get him out there and get to know the real him. You'll see he's a good guy."

"No, no," Gilbert said, playing it down just right, pulling her in. "I don't camp."

"It's the only time Trent's himself, happy," she said. "You might like it, Gilbert. You might even find you like *him* when he's out there."

Gilbert paused. *I doubt that*, he thought. He hated himself for what he was doing. He always thought of his poker talents—bluffing, plotting, reading, not only people, but their actions, even through a computer screen in an online poker game—as a superpower, to be used with great prudence and responsibility. It was a joke mostly, between Jeannie and him. But nonetheless, he vowed never to use his powers against his friends and loved ones.

But, tonight, here he was.

CHAPTER 64 | OCCUPIED

WITH AN EYE out for the mountain lion, Gilbert scrambled up the front steps and up to the front door on all fours. Despite his frantic hurry, he noticed something was off as soon as he reached the porch. The porch was empty. Not a chair or mat or table.

Gilbert crawled to the front door and started pounding.

There was no sign of life within. The house remained quiet and dark. No light came on. No footsteps came to the door.

There was no one home.

But the house would have a phone, he reasoned to himself. They would have a pantry with food, some kind of food. Gilbert banged on the door a few more times, and when the house remained quiet, he reached up for the door handle and grabbed it, to see if he could break the handle or the lock. But as he grabbed the handle, it turned, and the door swung open.

"Oh, God, thank you," Gilbert said to himself and crawled across the threshold and slammed the door closed, collapsing to the floor. "Thank you!"

But as the door slammed closed, there was a crash from inside the house.

Gilbert flipped over onto his stomach. "Hello?" he called out into the dark house. "Hello?"

He pulled himself onto all fours and then up to his feet, using the wall as a support. With weak and shaky steps, he hugged the wall and made his way toward the sound in the back of the house.

"I'm injured," he called out into the darkness. "Is someone here? Please help. I'm badly injured."

But there was no response.

Gilbert used the wall as support and was halfway across the first room he entered before he realized that the whole room was empty. There wasn't a piece of furniture anywhere.

"Hello," he called out again, his voice betraying the fact that he no longer expected to hear a friendly or helpful voice calling back. "Who's in there?" he yelped. He stopped as he reached the door into the kitchen, where he'd heard the sound.

CHAPTER 65 | HISTORY

THE SMELL OF dry rot was in the air: wood and dust. Beside the doorway to the darkened kitchen in the old, empty house in the woods, Gilbert hesitated.

More movement inside.

He was shaking and weak, but he took a deep breath, and another.

He planned to jump out in a strong fighting stance. He planned to be brave.

But as he made himself jump out into the doorway, it became much more of a peek than a jump, and as he did, he suddenly beheld black eyes inside the door staring back at him from only inches away. Around the black eyes were white rings, and behind that was the rest of the furry raccoon, right down to the ringed tail.

Gilbert jumped, maybe even higher than if it really had been a sharp-toothed psychopath with a club ambushing him from the dark kitchen—that being the last thought that crossed his mind as he jumped, or peeked, out into the doorway. As it was, the raccoon caught sight of him, and they locked eyes, and the raccoon made a jump for it, right across Gilbert's face, down to the counter and down to the floor, then off to wherever raccoons go.

The encounter nearly succeeded in stopping Gilbert's heart for good, and Gilbert pressed his forehead against the doorframe as the pounding in his chest plunged knives deeper and deeper into the pit of his brain. It felt like his sluggish brain was vibrating, like razor-filled Jell-O on a subwoofer.

It took him a few minutes to regain his strength, to focus enough to continue into the kitchen to find the pantry. But just like the first room, he found the pantry and the rest of the place empty. And he soon found the diorama. It was on an old wooden table, and it showed a historic scene of tiny little cows and pigs and chickens in and behind a barn. There were tiny little trees, and tiny little people, and this tiny little house. It told of a time when Great Camp Santanoni was up and running, catering to the country's elite fleeing the steaming cities of the eastern seaboard for a vacation up into the wild and untamed Adirondack mountains. This diorama showed the farm section and the house he was standing in, where the employees lived and worked and raised crops and animals for the kitchens and smokehouses in the enormous Great Camp lodge on Newcomb Lake.

The diorama showed Gilbert life in the nineteenth

century, in miniaturized form, and his own death in present day, in cinematic scope. This place was a museum in a ghost lodge. And there would be no food.

CHAPTER 66 | GATES

GILBERT STUMBLED OUT the front door, off the porch, and into the rain. The other buildings along the road were all part of the historic conservation, old and wooden, but well built. Placards out front. Inviting.

The smack, smack, smack of heavy drops of rain dripping from the giant trees in the front yard of the house landed on his pounding head and chased him down the steps and across the lawn to the dirt road. He reached the opening of the road and sloshed down into the mud on all fours. He scanned around himself, aware of the cat that must still be out there.

He crawled most of the way to the final bridge. The last river to cross before the main road. At times, he tried to stumble along on two legs but usually fell back to the ground with enough force to make the walking not worth the pain of the falling. The fastest he could travel was on all fours, one hand, one leg, one hand, one leg, one, two, three, four, one, two, three, four. He checked his surroundings as much as he could.

He didn't see or hear the cat again.

He crawled and crawled, dragging himself along the dirt road cutting through the thick Adirondack forest. The sun rose—or the sky became a lighter shade of gray on the other side of the clouds. The rain was letting up again though, coming down in little more than a sprinkle by then. But the ground was saturated with all the rain from the previous days, and the puddles and pools of mud stayed on the surface of everything.

On the trees, the first leaves of fall were turning in the coming daylight. Soon the forest would be blanketed in red and orange and yellow, a color extravaganza made grander with this long, cool drink of hurricane rain.

Gilbert reached a clearing and stopped. There were more houses, another cluster.

But Gilbert didn't get his hopes up this time. He'd seen a sign at a trailhead along the road that said the "Gatekeeper's Complex" was ahead in the direction he was crawling. The gate. The end. Where the noble carriages would have been met by the gatekeeper, a jovial and capable soul, no doubt. He would have lived right there at the entrance, ensuring that any weary travelers pulling their teams into the great lodge late at night or early in the morning would be received well and promptly—and the riffraff would be kept at bay.

But that was years ago, over a century ago. Today, the lot in front of the gatekeeper's house was an Adirondack Park parking lot for the vehicles of hikers and tourists visiting the historic site when it was open—which it was not.

Gilbert assessed the buildings in the cluster and wrote them off as useless, continuing his slog toward the bridge and the highway not far beyond. By then, Gilbert could hear more and more of the awful sound that had encompassed this whole affair: the rush of water.

When he heard it coming from the direction he was crawling, his stomach twisted into a knot. *That fucking sound!* The growing roar of water in front of him made all the smaller splashes and torrents washing all around him that much worse, that much more incessant. He thought about how many hours and days in a row he'd heard that sound: the drop and rush of water. *God, make it stop!* he pleaded in his aching head. It became harder and harder to concentrate on anything else. He shook his head and covered his ears, trying to will the water to stop falling for just a second, just a moment to let his head rest, to let his ears rest—just a moment. But no matter how hard he plugged his ears and tucked his head into himself, he couldn't make all that water stop running and racing all around him, down, down, down.

After the engulfing roar of the river, the next best clue that there was something wrong with the old bridge ahead was the orange highway barrier across the river, blocking people from driving up to the bridge from the other direction. Gilbert saw the roadblock barrier before he could see the flat of the bridge.

The large rounded steel supports that looked like the top of giant steel wheels rose above the gap, but the parallel steel wheels were pointing slightly to the right of the road beyond the river. When he crawled up closer, his fears were realized. The stone and block buttress on the other side of the river had been undermined by the river. The bridge and buttress held together, but the water had cut behind and below, and from the end of the moaning bridge, the water ran in a fifteen-foot swath out of the bank and through the road behind. It was now a bridge to nowhere, a pier angled into the rushing river.

Gilbert crawled all the way to the end of the pier and looked down at the thick muddy water rushing a few feet below. It was an impossible distance across to the other side.

THE LAST

GILBERT FLOPPED TO the pavement on the bridge and rolled over and lay on his back, looking up at the dizzying gray sky sliding overhead. This was the end of the line. A main country road through the Adirondacks was just a half a mile away. And though all he could hear was the never-ending, monotonous roar of the water below, he could almost imagine that he heard cars driving on that road. Maybe full of tourists up from the downstate cities to canoe the majestic lakes of the old Gooley Club, or to hike in the high peaks of the Adirondack Mountains—peaks whose old and mysterious summits hide in the clouds or rise above them on mornings like this, basking in the sunshine over a white sea engulfing the quiet towns and hamlets below. The heartiest locals would no doubt be up by then, driving their old pickups and bakery vans through the morning fog, waving to their neighbors as they headed off to a fishing hole or their first delivery, the mountains bearing quiet witness to it all, generations coming and going, grown and buried in that same rich soil. He could practically feel the rumble of the pickups. They were right there. So close. He knew it. But there was a bend in the access road across the river, and all he could see was the thick forest beyond it.

Gilbert looked back up at the sky. On it went, over and over and over, perpetually careless. Just like the river in front of him. Away they both raced to another place, chasing some hidden force across the universe and passing, with blatant disregard, every Gilbert Willards in the world along the way. The sky kept rolling, and the river kept running, and Gilbert lay on his back and looked up at the one and listened to the other. *Here I am*, he thought, *like a peg in a blizzard. Turn this rain to snow and cover me over. The mice will eat me in the spring. Or let the mountain lion return and have me tonight. It is a fact*, he thought.

He looked up at the rain falling down on his face. This was where he would die, on a flooded bridge a half mile from rescue. He couldn't help but think that it was exactly what he deserved. He'd just killed a man. He was attacked. But maybe he wanted to be attacked. Maybe he wanted to kill Trent from the inception. Maybe he lured him out into the woods with that intention, facts or not. And maybe dying right there on that spot was what he deserved.

As he drifted, he suddenly heard footsteps behind him on the bridge. He snapped his head up to look as fast as he could muster in his state, and there above him stood Buck.

"Tough luck," Buck said, nodding to the bridge, not even saying hello.

"Help me," Gilbert croaked.

Buck just took a deep breath and looked down at Gilbert. "How did you think this was all gonna work out?"

"Help me."

"Have you seen the cat?"

Gilbert blinked his eyes, shutting them tight, and then opened them and looked around himself. His mind was moving like molasses. He strained to understand what Buck had asked him. "Not for a while."

"That's good, then," Buck said.

"Buck, help me, please," Gilbert pleaded and reached up to him. "How do we get across?"

"Why are you out here, Gilbert?"

Gilbert slumped back to the ground. "I did what had to be done."

Buck just raised his one eyebrow and looked out into the forest. He stood without speaking for a long time.

"Please," Gilbert said.

Buck scratched his grizzled chin and chuckled, then reached inside his long black trench coat and pulled out a pack of cigarettes and a box of matches.

Gilbert watched in stunned wonder as Buck casually pulled out a cigarette and stuck it in his mouth. Then he opened the sliding box of wooden matches and pulled one out, taking a deep breath as he looked down at the ground, as if thinking hard about something. He stayed there for a long moment without striking the match.

Gilbert didn't even know what to say. "You have cigarettes?" he croaked, eventually.

"Ever seen James Brown at the Apollo?" Buck said, disregarding Gilbert's question.

Gilbert took a moment to process the words. "In person?"

"No, not in person, you idiot. Probably VHS if I had to guess," he said, mostly to himself.

"No," Gilbert said.

"Good stuff." He nodded his head and smiled as he thought about it. Then he chuckled once and struck the match on the side of the matchbook and brought the flame to the end of his cigarette, taking a long pull as the red tip of the cigarette glowed. He exhaled the smoke in a long, satisfied breath that hung in the drizzling rain.

Gilbert smelled the smoke and found it oddly pleasant. He'd never smoked. Tried it once in high school and never wanted to try it again. But for some reason, he was grateful for that smell as he lay there on his back, looking up at Buck, the road he'd crawled down stretching back into the forest, past the gatekeeper's house and the stable and the rectangular dirt parking lot and the placards and historical markers—and the scene of the killing. Behind it all, Santanoni Peak rose in the distance above the tops of the trees, where the road disappeared, the thinning clouds obscuring all but glimpses of its ridgeline.

Gilbert dropped his head to the ground and breathed in the cigarette smell. He took two deep breaths of the sweet, smoky air with his eyes closed, savoring it, and when he opened his eyes, Buck was gone.

"Buck?" Gilbert said, suddenly very scared. "Buck?"

But there was no answer.

Gilbert could still smell the cigarette and he pushed himself up into a more seated position and scanned the area on that side of the river. He saw nothing. Buck was gone. Just like that. He could still smell the cigarette. Gilbert scanned the area in every direction. Nothing.

But when he looked behind himself toward the broken end of the bridge, his eye caught the sight of something blue, manmade, across the river. Then, as he focused, he saw that just fifty yards away, up the river a little bit, sat a boy of about fourteen in a blue rain jacket, resting on a stump and looking out at the flooded river, smoking a cigarette.

Gilbert couldn't believe his eyes. He blinked hard, and then again, and there was no change in the lonely boy, out sneaking a cigarette by the river. It took a long moment for Gilbert to come around, to believe it was real, and then to know what to do, to make a sign, to call out.

With all the effort he had, he raised an arm and waved it.

The boy didn't see him at first. But eventually, he caught sight, and when he did, he jumped up off the stump and threw his cigarette down instinctively, looking down at it as if he could will the situation to be that the cigarette didn't exist and he hadn't been caught doing anything.

But Gilbert watched as the boy's face quickly turned from worry about being caught to worry about what he was seeing. He took two steps back and looked like he was about to run. But Gilbert waved to him as frantically as he could, pleading with him through hand gestures and expression to not run away. The boy hesitated, then stayed—timidly.

Any croaking shout that Gilbert could muster was obviously being swallowed up by the river rushing between them. When it was clear that the boy could not hear him, Gilbert resorted to hand signals, holding his thumb and pinky out to make a hand phone, holding it to his ear with a questioning look on his face.

The boy nodded his head, understanding the question and pulling out a cell phone from his pocket. The boy unlocked the phone and started to punch in a number, presumably 9-1-1. But as he did, Gilbert waved his arms vigorously from across the river, telling him to stop.

The boy stopped and looked at Gilbert with an uncertain tilt to his head.

Gilbert held up his hand to ask the boy to bear

with him, then he started making numbers with his fingers. The boy furrowed his eyebrow at first, not understanding, but then he nodded his head and realized what Gilbert was trying to ask him: to call a number, a specific number.

GILBERT WAS NEVER heard from again. His body was never found. After an expansive search, the authorities found the canoe further down Cold River from Gilbert and Trent's last known camp. They also found the sleeping bags they threw over while trying to cross Calahan Brook, and they found tracks in the historical home Gilbert entered. But they never found either of them alive again. Trent's bones were found two years later, outside what looked to have been an animal's den at one time, only a quarter mile from the road. But not Gilbert's.

Those among us less swayed by the heart might think that maybe that boy smoking the cigarette didn't even exist, just like Buck, and that Gilbert's dead body probably joined his ill-fated and ill-intentioned traveling companion in the secret den of that mountain lion, where the two of them provided some much-needed extra units of protein to the winter diet of that momma cat and her growing cubs—all very real, if you believe what some experts say about the photos from the den where Trent was found.

Perhaps someday evidence of Gilbert will be found. Perhaps his bones will also show up, chewed on by those previously undiscovered animals repopulating into that dark green abyss of mountain wilderness in northern New York: the Adirondack Mountains, where monsters be.

But there are some more-optimistic folks among us who point to a few oddities that we should make note of here. Gilbert was never found, as we said. But oddly, Jeannie—and Snowball—also disappeared, after packing a few of their most important belongings and emptying their bank accounts. And further, while Doctor Zimmer mourned the loss of the new head of his pediatric hospital, that hospital has received a modest anonymous donation every year on the day of Jeannie and Gilbert's disappearance. And while Gilbert and Jeannie's little blue Toyota was never found, Jeannie's cell phone pinged a cell tower in northwestern Montana five days later. It only registered for a second, then was gone. That cell ping was the last known trace of Jeannie and Gilbert.

Some think the mob got them and they're both feeding record lake trout at the bottom of Long Lake or Lake George. But our optimistic friends like to point out that right around this time, a certain, poor, fourteen-year-old boy who lived near the bridge to Great Camp Santanoni suddenly came up with enough money to buy himself a new dirt bike that he flaunted around town all year. They find this odd, and they believe, as do I, that Jeannie and Gilbert paid that boy to keep his mouth shut and then fled, Jeannie nursing Gilbert back to health and the two of them living under assumed names somewhere quiet—happy and in love.

According to the official report, both men died in the forest. The evidence Gilbert sent to the police helped bring down Jimmy Dove and his crew, and Jimmy Dove brought down much of the Bogacci family. Not Chuck, though, interestingly. In fact, the FBI claims to not know anyone fitting that name or description. You can read into that what you will.

As for Gilbert, he was declared a hero, touted for sacrificing himself in the name of justice, and "posthumously" awarded a number of merits for his act.

Gilbert Willards, they said, the gambler hero who risked it all.

AUTHOR'S POSTSCRIPT

THE CONTENTS OF this story were told to me by a traveler, late at night, inside a diner on the western prairie. While I cannot attest to the veracity of this tale, looking into the eyes of the teller, I believe it to be true, and that I met Gilbert Willards himself, by the hands of fate.

But we will never know.

THE END

HURRICANE CANOE

An Adirondack Wilderness Thriller

Richard M. Brock

*

If you enjoyed this story, please share, recommend, or review. Every mention helps and is greatly appreciated.

#hurricanecanoe

www.richardmbrock.com

facebook.com/richardmbrockauthor

ACKNOWLEDGEMENTS

WITH THIS TALE concluded, I'd like to send a special thank you to my mother for, well, being my mother, first and foremost, and for her tireless work on this story and all my other writings. I love you, Momma. Thank you for everything. I'd also like to send a special thanks to my father, to whom this book is dedicated and from whom I received much of my storyteller's spirit. Love you, Pops. And of course, big thanks to my brother and sister, who *always* have my back. Thank you to the rest of my friends and family for your continuous feedback and support. I can't list you all, but I appreciate you. To my Aunt Linda: thank you for your help on this story and for inspiring me always. Thank you to my Kickstarter backers for your generous belief; I hope you enjoyed your story. A giant thank you to my readers, of course: my collaborators. Without you, the story wouldn't ever be a story. You add the magic. And finally, the greatest earthly thanks to my wife, Erin, for being here and being there and being all things in all ways, all the time. I love you.

BACKERS BACK PAGE

EXTRA SPECIAL THANKS to these wonderful people who helped bring this book to life; I am forever grateful:

Andrew Butt

Sheila Brock

Jack Brock

Shannon Brock

Lucas Brock

Shereen Brock

Linda Mead

MaryAnn Pendergrass

Thomas Davenport

Thank you!

ABOUT THE AUTHOR

RICHARD M. BROCK IS the author of the acclaimed blues thriller, *Cross Dog Blues*, as well as the picaresque adventure, *Up a Tree*, and the all-new wilderness thriller, *Hurricane Canoe*. Lauded by *Kirkus Reviews* as "true brilliance" and "an exhilarating exercise in suspense," his novels have an average Amazon review of over 4.5 stars. Originally from the Adirondack Mountains of upstate New York, he and his wife now live in Colorado.

Follow along at facebook.com/richardmbrockauthor or learn more at www.richardmbrock.com.

www.richardmbrock.com

www.ingramcontent.com/pod-product-compliance
Lightning Source LLC
Chambersburg PA
CBHW030140310726
48970CB00005B/1516